ZONE ZERO

Western powers plan to explode a hydrogen bomb in a remote area of Southern Algeria — code named Zone Zero. The zone has to be evacuated. Fort Ney is the smallest Foreign Legion outpost in the zone, commanded by a young lieutenant. Here, too, is the English legionnaire, tortured by previous cowardice, as well as a little Greek who has within him the spark of greatness. It has always been a peaceful place — until the twelve travellers arrive. Now the outwitted garrison faces the uttermost limit of horror . . .

JOHN ROBB

ZONE ZERO

Complete and Unabridged

LINFORD
Leicester

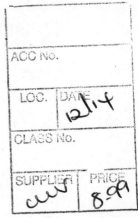

First published in Great Britain

First Linford Edition
published 2014

A catalogue record for this book is available
from the British Library.

ISBN 978–1–4448–2232–8

Published by
F. A. Thorpe (Publishing)
Anstey, Leicestershire

Set by Words & Graphics Ltd.
Anstey, Leicestershire
Printed and bound in Great Britain by
T. J. International Ltd., Padstow, Cornwall

This book is printed on acid-free paper

PART ONE

(JUNE 26–JULY 1)

1

Evacuation

General Jonot unrolled the map of Algeria. He pinned it flat to the table. The staff officers gathered round to examine it. They concentrated on a neatly pencilled square which enclosed part of the Territory of the Oases. The general pointed to it with a well-manicured finger.

'Evacuation,' he announced. 'Complete and absolute evacuation. Every man, woman and child must be removed from the area. There can be no exceptions.'

An elderly and faded colonel said: 'It will be difficult. The area covers a hundred square miles.'

'I am aware of both those facts,' General Jonot said tartly.

The colonel flushed. But he was not deterred. He added: 'The Arabs will resent it very much. We may move them from the zone, but can we be sure they

3

will not drift back?'

'They will probably die if they do. That will be explained to them.'

There was an uneasy shuffle among the operational staff officers. Some went on looking at the map. Some looked at each other. None looked at the general.

The colonel cleared his throat.

'But, *mon generale*, they will not understand.'

'Understand? I don't see why not. Surely the choice between life and death is simple enough!'

There was a touch of asperity in General Jonot's tones. But the colonel — who was due to retire shortly — was not intimidated. He voiced his doubts with the quiet indifference of a man who has nothing to gain or lose.

'The Arabs may not see it in such a simple light, *mon generale*. They are primitive and peaceful peoples and they have a strong attachment to their villages. How can we expect them to understand when we tell them about the great explosion? We can tell them that the Western powers are going to detonate the

4

first of the new fission bombs in the area
... we can say that a hundred square miles of desert will be dangerous for weeks afterwards ... we can talk to them of the deadly gamma rays ... but they will not comprehend. They will know only that they have been uprooted.'

Some of the officers gave a cautious mumble of assent. General Jonot shrugged.

'We have our orders,' he said. 'We must carry them out.'

An intellectual-looking captain blinked nervously behind his horn spectacles. His voice squeaked somewhat as he said: 'It will do us much harm, *mon generale*.'

Jonot glared through him. He did not encourage contributions from junior officers.

'Will it? I am sorry to hear that. But I think we will survive.'

The captain withdrew in confusion. But the colonel took up his point.

'No doubt he means that the Legion will suffer, in terms of good will. Under our protection the Arabs have lived in peace for many years and they are grateful. But they will hate us — *oui*, hate us — when we eject items from their homes.'

For a moment, General Jonot was silent. Then he said: 'These things are soon forgotten. Don't forget that arrangements are being made to look after the displaced Arabs. A reception camp is being built near Tuggurt where they will be housed and fed until it is safe for them to return.'

The colonel smiled coldly.

'Return?' he queried. 'Return to what? If what we hear about the bomb is true, most of them will have nothing to come back to. Their villages will have disintegrated.'

'They will be compensated.'

'With what, *generale*? Money? They have little use for coinage.'

Jonot shrugged and suddenly he looked tired. He *was* tired. Secretly, he knew that the objections were valid ones. But, because of his rank, he could not say so. He attempted an oblique defence.

'*I* am not responsible for this decision,' he said. 'It was decided by the Western governments that Algeria was the best place for the explosion. And remember, *mes officiers*, that a great honour now falls on the French Foreign Legion, for we have been entrusted entirely with the security arrangements . . . '

Jonot paused and surveyed the group of worried faces. Then he added: 'Discontented Arabs will not be our only problem. Many skilful enemy agents will certainly try to approach the explosion area — for certain powers are most curious about the bomb. We must see to it that they learn nothing.'

He thrust papers into his despatch case. The conference was over. They were all relieved. The colonel said tentatively: 'Will you take a glass of wine, *mon generale*?'

Jonot shook his head then put on his silver-corded hat.

'Thank you no. I must return to the command centre at once. But there is one more matter I must mention, gentlemen. There is a code name for the explosion area. In future it will be called Zone Zero. Don't forget that. It is vitally important. Zone Zero . . . '

2

The Fort

The vultures (it was claimed) laughed when they looked down on Fort Ney. They opened their cruel beaks and gave full-bodied squawks of amusement. Practically every legionnaire who had ever served in the place was adamant on the point.

They could have been right.

Fort Ney was a vicious joke. It was an insult to the memory of a great soldier. It was also an insult to the legionnaires who lived within its narrow walls.

It was not really a fort. It was a tiny stone box with half a lid. A place of red sandstone where men sweated and cursed, argued and slept. Where with complete impartiality they called upon God and the Devil to free them from their infernal boredom.

It had been adapted from an ancient

Saracen outpost. But the adaptation had been meagre.

The puny eight-foot-tall ramparts were unchanged. So were the centuries-old wood and iron gates which were nearly useless as a barrier.

Only two structural changes had been made since the Legion took over. One was the erection of a stone building in the centre of the tiny compound. Here the garrison slept and ate. And here the officer commanding had his office, which also served as a bunk and radio room. The other alteration was purely symbolic. It consisted of a flagpole which supported a listless Tricolour.

The High Command referred to Fort Ney as a 'prestige base'.

It was admitted that the place could never resist a determined attack. But it never had been attacked — so why worry about that? Standing on the southern extremity of the Territory of the Oases, Fort Ney brooded maternally over a handful of scattered and contented Arab villages.

Once — many years back — a

committee of the High Command had discussed a proposal to evacuate the fort. The idea had been dismissed contemptuously. Such a move, it was decided, would result in loss of face among the Arabs.

And so at regular intervals of three months a relief column of thirty men under a lieutenant marched miserably over a hundred miles of desert to take over the fort.

Lieutenant Andre D'Aran's garrison had arrived four days ago.

Four days. More than eighty days to go before they would be able to return to the comparative comforts of the barracks at Tala Baku.

D'Aran sat on the corner of his hard bunk and ruminated darkly.

This, he told himself, was the worst period of all. It was the time when a man wanted to weep over the past and lament the fact that he had no future. This was the time when the atmosphere alternated between bovine apathy and simmering fury.

The time when discipline — necessarily informal in such a confined place

— suffered great strain.

D'Aran glowered at his cell-like room. A narrow shaft of sunlight coming through the open window played upon the desk in the corner. It was an untidy desk, well littered with a profusion of garrison reports. On the floor beside it there stood a massive and aged typewriter.

He turned his attention to the trestle table against the opposite wall. Here, in the shadow, there was a bewildering array of wires, knobs and valves which comprised the fort's radio receiving and transmitting set. He was supposed to use this once a week to tap out a routine report to Tala Baku. But D'Aran knew from past experience that the instrument seldom worked properly because the intense heat soon dried the power out of the batteries. Sometimes it took a couple of days' hard tapping before one was able to transmit the two words 'All Correct' to Baku. Then, in all probability, there would be another day of agonised listening with the headphones on before one picked up the reply 'Signal Acknowledged'.

D'Aran sighed. He rose slowly from his bunk, rubbing his seat. He crossed to a tarnished wall mirror and inspected himself in it.

He saw a young and intelligent face which was prematurely lined at the corners of the mouth. He saw large grey eyes which had once sparkled with happiness, but which did so no longer. He saw curly black hair which needed the application of brush and comb.

'Andre,' he told himself harshly, 'you're a damned fool! In three months you'll return to Tala Baku and you'll be arrested. And when the whole story comes out . . . you'll go to prison . . . '

He grimaced at his reflection. Then he added: 'In the meantime you have the three months to think about it . . . and about her . . . '

D'Aran hesitated. Then he groped in his tunic breast pocket. He pulled out what had once been an entire photograph. But now it was like a carelessly assembled jigsaw puzzle. For, in a moment of jealous desperation, he had torn the picture into many pieces. And, when he was calm again, he had pieced them together and pasted them to a sheet of paper. The result was not flattering to Lucinne. But her dark, tempestuous beauty could still be detected. And D'Aran's memory supplied the rest.

He fingered the distorted portrait tenderly. His care-worn face relaxed, and he whispered: 'I think you were worth it . . . '

Lieutenant D'Aran was still gazing at the picture when Sergeant Vogel knocked and came in.

Vogel saluted correctly but indifferently.

'*Mon officier*,' he announced in French, which was heavily laden with Dutch vowels, 'some men on horseback are approaching from the north.'

At first D'Aran regarded the bulky sergeant with distaste. He had been almost happy in his reverie.

'Well? That's not very unusual, is it?'

The phlegmatic Vogel was unmoved.

'They are *not* Arabs, *mon officier*,' he said with heavy emphasis.

D'Aran looked at his sergeant with new interest.

'Not Arabs! Then who are they?'

'They seem to be white men, but I am not sure. They are still some distance away. I counted twelve of them.'

D'Aran picked up his kepi and fastened his tunic buttons. Then, after a brief search, he found his binoculars in his valise. He slung them over his shoulders and strode out, Vogel following.

The sunlight in the open compound was blinding. D'Aran shielded his eyes as he crossed to the north wall and mounted the few steps to the ridiculously low ramparts. Two legionnaires were on duty here. They were staring across the sand.

The legionnaires on the other ramparts were also staring north. There was an atmosphere of repressed expectancy.

D'Aran stared through the glasses, fumbling with the focus wheel. He whistled under his breath as he saw the approaching horsemen. They were no more than a mile off, and their details could easily be seen. Sergeant Vogel had been right. They were not Arabs. Their skins were white — almost startlingly so. As if they were strangers to the desert.

They rode good and tough animals. The twelve of them were stretched out in a precise line. It was odd, that line. It was almost like the slow, walking approach of cavalry. It was disciplined in a way one would not expect from men who were dressed in civilian alpaca suits and rather old-fashioned pith helmets.

Vogel said: 'They must have travelled a long way, *mon officier*. They've brought four pack-mules. And they have a spare horse.'

D'Aran raised his glasses very slightly and saw the mules. They were heavily laden.

He said: 'Why are they out here? There's nothing to interest civilians in this area.'

Vogel said: 'I think we'll soon know the answer. They must be intending to visit us.'

'Whether they intend to visit us or not is beside the point,' D'Aran muttered. 'They are civilians and we are responsible for their safety, so I must know where they are going and if they are capable of finding their way. If they get lost in this

15

area I will be held responsible, and . . . '

He broke off. He suddenly realised that his conduct in the fort was not likely to concern the Legion much in future. Already the news of his crime might be circulating through Tala Baku. Already orders might have been given for his arrest on his return. His military future was certain to be brief. All because of what he did for her . . .

With an effort, D'Aran subdued the thought. He dropped the binoculars in their leather case and said: 'Sergeant Vogel — you'd better walk out and meet these people. Present them with my compliments and ask them into the fort.'

Vogel nodded and saluted. When he had gone, D'Aran wondered why he had given the order. On the face of it, it was a stupid one, even though it might be explained on the ground of courtesy. It was very unlikely that the travellers would attempt to ignore the only military base (and the only white habitation) within sixty miles.

Yet some instinct had compelled him to send Vogel out there. An instinct which

16

knew no reason. Unless . . . unless it was that he wanted to see what the travellers would do when the sergeant approached them.

Oui! That was it! D'Aran found himself facing an unpleasant truth. He was not merely puzzled by the appearance of the twelve white men. He was also uneasy about it. He had a feeling, growing steadily stronger, that all was far from well.

From his slight elevation he watched Vogel stride through the open gates. He had a sense of the dramatic, had Vogel. He had donned a red-lined sergeant's dress cape for the occasion. And he had substituted a braided kepi for his sun-faded cap.

D'Aran gazed after him for a while. Then, to rest his eyes, he glanced round the compound. He was surprised and mildly annoyed. Being early afternoon, the entire garrison, except those on guard duty, were supposed to be resting. But most of the legionnaires had left their bunks and had mounted the north ramparts at a respectful distance from

17

D'Aran. All of them were improperly dressed. Some had not even bothered to put on their tunics, and their tanned bodies glittered as they lounged against the stonework.

For a moment D'Aran thought of ordering them away. But he dismissed the idea, for the men's curiosity was understandable. And in a tiny fort such as this, the commanding officer (if he was wise) closed his eyes to many things which would be intolerable in a larger and less isolated base.

He looked again towards Vogel and the horsemen. They were less than half a mile distant and only a few yards separated them.

He saw the horsemen draw rein. He saw Vogel salute as a sudden gust of hot breeze revealed the redness within his cape.

D'Aran raised his glasses again and watched the travellers form a semi-circle round Vogel. They were talking. He could detect the head and arm movements which accompany conversation. Then, like the opening of a fan, the horsemen spread out and started again towards the fort. Vogel — a dwarfed and unimportant-looking Vogel — was walking in the centre.

D'Aran studied the sergeant. There was a satisfied expression on his large, florid face. He was looking upwards and talking happily to the man on his left.

Then D'Aran made a closer inspection of the horsemen.

There was something about them . . .

All of them were big men. All hard-looking men. They did not look like a party of normal civilians, despite their pallor. And they held themselves very straight in the saddle.

Now the binoculars were no longer necessary. They were less than a couple of hundred yards away. He could hear the slow crunching of hooves and the faint jingle of bridle chains.

D'Aran turned and walked thoughtfully down the steps. He took up a position just inside the gates. As he waited he sensed that the legionnaires were watching him.

The horsemen halted immediately

outside. The scent of the sweating animals spread heavily on the air. Vogel stepped forward, sweating under his cape. He smiled as he saluted.

'An expedition, *mon officier*,' he declared.

'A what!'

One of the travellers laughed politely. Then he dismounted in a single, easy movement. He came towards D'Aran with an outstretched hand. He spoke fluent French with only a faint and indeterminate accent.

'Please don't look so surprised, lieutenant! I am Doctor Gallast, and this is the Cracow University archaeological research party. We are making for the Sanna Oasis and we hope you will be able to give us shelter for the night.'

D'Aran took the open hand. The grip was as strong as his own.

He met the man's eyes. Cold eyes. They did not reflect the smile which creased his large, darkly stubbled features.

D'Aran gave his name. Then said: 'I'll certainly do what I can for you, but as you can see, there's very little room here.'

'I understand. You are a small garrison.'

'Only thirty.'

D'Aran silently cursed himself immediately he had spoken. The information on the strength of his garrison was not strictly secret. In fact, it would be fairly obvious to anyone who studied the dimensions of Fort Ney or considered the fact that a mere lieutenant held the command. But there was no reason why he should give the answer so easily.

Gallast made a deprecating gesture.

'Then we are sorry to trouble you. But if you would allow us to pitch our tents in your compound . . . the walls would give us some protection from the night winds.'

D'Aran did not answer the question. Instead he said: 'I didn't know there was anything to interest archaeologists at the Sanna Oasis.'

'Then you are mistaken, lieutenant. It is known that there are ancient Saracen remains there, although they have not been excavated. We are to make a preliminary survey.'

D'Aran nodded and thought quickly.

He knew that occasional scientific expeditions went out into the desert, but he had never before heard of one visiting this area. Still, if these people wanted to dig at Sanna it was their business — so long as they did nothing to disturb the Arabs there. But he could not get rid of that haunting doubt — the feeling that something was wrong . . .

He said diffidently: 'Are all of your party archaeologists?'

'Ah, yes,' Gallast said pleasantly. 'But of course this is an arduous undertaking, so, as you can see, all of us are young and strong.'

'Where have you come from?'

'We came to North Africa by way of Oran. Then we flew to Tala Baku. From there we have progressed by horseback and we are glad the journey is nearly over.'

He spoke calmly — perhaps a little too calmly. D'Aran said: 'As a formality, I will have to see your passports.'

'Certainly. They are with the baggage on the mules. You will find them in order.'

'I'll look at them later. Meantime, you

are welcome to camp in the compound. But I'm afraid there is little I can do for you in the way of hospitality.'

They talked for a few more minutes while the horsemen entered the fort. Then D'Aran was introduced to them. Like their leader, they spoke French. But they were stolid, uncommunicative. After a party of legionnaires had been detailed to help with the tents, D'Aran went thoughtfully back to his room. Gallast had arranged to call on him in ten minutes with the passports.

★ ★ ★

A call signal was buzzing faintly through the radio head phones. D'Aran heard it immediately as he entered the room. He was surprised. It was unusual — a signal to be received outside the routine hours. And it was extraordinary that it should come through at such power.

He sat at the table, whisked off his cap, put on the phones. Then he pulled the Morse key towards him, giving an answering recognition call.

There was no difficulty about receiving this message. Each long and short buzz was of pristine clarity. D'Aran's pencil flew over his pad of paper as he took down the letters. In three minutes it was finished. He tapped out an acknowledgment. Then he went to the desk. He unlocked a drawer, took out a slim, leather-bound cipher book. With that at his elbow he started to decode.

The first few words gave him a minor shock. The message had been transmitted direct from the Legion staff headquarters at Sidi Bel Abbes.

No wonder it had been received so easily! The military radio station there was the most powerful in all French Africa.

D'Aran felt a quiver of excitement as he worked. And his hands were shaking when he finally threw down the pencil and read the result.

From secretary to High Command, Sidi Bel Abbes. To officer commanding Fort Ney. Priority absolute. Thermonuclear test explosion to take place near Sanna

Oasis at 15.00 hours, July 8. All civil populations in your command area to be evacuated by midnight July 4 and directed to Tuggurt reception camp. Danger area known as Zone Zero. Extent: 100 miles square from latitude 20 and longitude 3. You will evacuate fort at 22.00 hours, July 6, and take up protective positions behind Keeba foothills . . .

There was more of it. It consisted of advice on how to dig in behind the hills (which lay thirty miles north of the fort) so as to avoid the enormous heat radiations. There was a warning to stay under cover for at least three days after the explosion. Then the garrison was to return to the fort and resume duty there — if it was habitable.

But if the fort had been destroyed by the explosion, they were to link up with K Company — a small legion force based some two days' march west. There they would receive further orders.

D'Aran's nervous tension gave way to bewilderment. Then annoyance. He had only a hazy knowledge of nuclear physics, but it was obvious that this was to be the most devastating man-made explosion ever attempted. Preparations for it must have been going on for months. Yet — since this was June 29th — he had been given less than nine days' notice . . .

And he had only a week in which to persuade several hundred scattered Arabs to move to the far distant Tuggurt — if they would be persuaded.

'Preposterous!' he said aloud. 'The Arabs will certainly give trouble. They won't understand. It can't be done in the time.'

But within him, he knew it would have to be done. And he realised that there were many other Legion outposts in Zone Zero which were almost certainly receiving similar orders at this very time. Each of them would have a commanding officer who was just as baffled and annoyed as he was.

There had been rumours of the explosion. He recalled hearing them when in Tala Baku. But he had not been much interested. They had been fragmentary and, he thought, unconvincing. In any case, he had had other matters on his mind. Lucinne, for instance, Lucinne and the fifty thousand francs he had stolen for her . . .

For the second time within an hour he had to force her from his mind. Her memory was like the remembered fragrance of last summer's flowers — still there, yet gone beyond recall.

He said: 'Let hell take all women!' But there was no conviction in his tones and he concentrated again on his immediate problems.

This nuclear explosion near the Sanna Oasis . . .

Sanna Oasis!

He jerked upright in his chair and stared fixedly at the bare wall. *Dieu!* Why hadn't he thought of it immediately? That was where Gallast and his archaeological party were going!

What a coincidence! But was it a coincidence? Could it be that they . . . ?

He recoiled from the unfinished thought. He did *not* want to indulge in melodramatics. But . . . but even if their papers were in order, they would have to be turned back without delay. In fact, he would probably have to detail half a dozen men to escort them out of Zone Zero. And he must inform the High Command of their presence. Obviously they ought not to have been allowed to proceed beyond Baku. There had been an administrative hitch somewhere.

There was a sharp double knock on the door. D'Aran mopped his greasy brow and muttered '*Entre*.'

Gallast came in.

He said: 'I have come to clear up any doubts you may have about us, lieutenant.' But he was not holding the passports. He was holding a Luger automatic pistol.

3

Observation Post

D'Aran opened his mouth to speak. But his vocal chords were temporarily paralysed and his mind had become a swirling haze of incredulous confusion. He gazed stupidly at the weapon which was levelled at the middle of his stomach. He continued to gaze at it as Gallast pulled over the chair from the radio table and sat opposite him.

Gallast said easily: 'Is this your administrative office?'

Still D'Aran did not answer. Gallast smiled.

'But obviously it is,' he added. 'It seems to be your living quarters, too. It is all somewhat cramped but we scarcely expected anything else. After all, it was the smallness of this place, as well as its geographical situation, which brought us here.'

D'Aran felt a clear click in his brain. It was as if a brake had been released from his mental motor. He jumped to his feet.

'What are you gibbering about? Have you gone mad? Put that gun away!'

Gallast thumbed free the safety catch and his forefinger took first pressure on the trigger. Both movements were clearly visible.

'Sit down, lieutenant. I don't want to kill you, but I shall if you do not do as I say.'

For perhaps five seconds D'Aran remained standing, his prematurely lined face twitching, his eyes wild. Then he sat heavily, like a man under a hypnotic compulsion. He knew that Gallast was not exaggerating.

He said slowly: 'I don't know what this is all about. But I warn you that it's both a military and civil offence to threaten me with a firearm. You will be arrested and handed to the commandant at Tala Baku.'

Gallast nodded. His free hand rubbed the thick black bristles on his chin.

'It's an academic warning, lieutenant.'

'*Tiens!* It's nothing of the sort. It's

30

completely practicable. I only hope for your own sake that you're suffering some mental disability. If you are not responsible for your actions, then the commandant may take a lenient view.'

'You are being insulting, lieutenant. I do not care to be insulted. I am trying to break it to you gently that the fort is no longer under your command and your garrison has been made helpless . . .'

He broke off to glance at a heavy strap watch. Then he added: 'If you'll listen, you'll hear something rather dramatic within half a minute . . .'

D'Aran listened, his mind abducted by the intensity of the man's words. The seconds passed slowly, heavily, like the footfalls of a man nearing the gallows.

Then he heard them.

He heard two almost simultaneous reverberations. Strong and cruel explosions which echoed weirdly against the fort walls. And he identified them immediately.

They were pistol shots. And from the east ramparts a man screamed.

Legionnaires Toto and Vakasky were on duty on the east ramparts.

It was an unfortunate combination, for the two men shared a smouldering distrust of each other. The cause, of course, was a woman. She was a massively stout lady of varied antecedents and flexible morals who lived in the native quarter of Baku. She was known as Anna.

Toto, who was impelled by the hot passions of his native Spain, had a deep affection for Anna. He regarded her as his exclusive property. It was unfortunate that Vakasky, a Russian from Georgia, regarded Anna in the same light. And each strongly resented the fact that he was compelled to share Anna's charms with the other. Each was determined to settle the intolerable situation before the garrison returned to Baku.

So it was that each time they passed each other on the ramparts a minor but significant crisis arose.

Vakasky — who was much the larger — contrived to get on the wall side as they approached. Then, when they were level, he attempted to nudge an indignant Toto off the ledge and on to the compound. The fact that he had not so far succeeded was probably due to the sparseness of opportunity. It was less than ten minutes since they had taken over the guard with the general relief and in that period the Russian had not been able to get his timing right. But there could be no doubt that ultimately he would have pushed Toto into eight feet of space.

Would have . . .

If they had not heard a sudden quiet but incisively spoken order from just below them.

It said: 'Drop your rifles, legionnaires!'

They looked down, forgetting their animosity. And they saw one of the archaeological party. He was aiming a heavy Luger gas-ejection pistol at them.

They stopped uncertainly, blinking at the weapon. Like children, who were seeing, yet not believing.

The man with the Luger gestured impatiently. He repeated the order, but this time with more volume, with additional emphasis.

The Russian and the Spaniard were immobile. They stood side by side on the ledge.

It was Vakasky who ultimately acted. He was a courageous man, was Legionnaire Vakasky. He was also a foolish one.

He tried to use his Lebel.

The rifle was in the orthodox *repos* position — suspended by the sling from the left shoulder. He attempted to free it as a necessary preliminary to squeezing the trigger.

Vakasky was still in the initial stages of sliding the weapon down his arm when the Luger was fired — twice.

The first bullet entered Vakasky's body at a point exactly one inch above his navel. His rifle clattered on to the stonework as he clutched at his belly. His face had suddenly become grey-blue, as though tinted by a colour filter. He opened his quivering lips. And he gave forth a scream which blended fury and agony. The sound faded into a choking sob as more blood rushed from a torn lung into his throat.

He toppled slowly and heavily forward, like a venerable tree in a gale. He crashed on to the compound's boot-hardened sand. And he lay there, face down, feebly kicking up the fine dust.

In a sense, Toto was more fortunate.

The bullet which killed him was almost simultaneous with that which hit Vakasky. It lodged in the top right side of his sleek head. The Spaniard was dead even as he revolved round, prior to slumping over the ramparts.

For a few seconds he remained balanced half in and half out of the fort. Then his body disappeared over the wall.

Six other legionnaires were on duty at that time — two on each of the three remaining walls.

They, also, were being menaced by men with Lugers.

And they saw what happened to their comrades Vakasky and Toto. They knew with a hollow, uncontradictable certainty, that they would share a similar fate if they attempted resistance.

So they did as they were ordered.

They dropped their Lebels.

They descended into the compound like sleepwalkers.

And, under guard, they formed into an astonished and incredulous little group.

★ ★ ★

Twenty-two legionnaires were in the compound building. They heard the Luger shots. But they did not pay much attention to them. They were trying to adjust themselves to more personal problems.

A few of them had helped the visitors to put up their tents. Then all had returned to their bunks to sweat out what was left of the compulsory rest period.

They lay in semi-nakedness.

They watched the grease ooze out of their bodies and into the unyielding straw mattresses.

They slapped wearily and ineffectually at the fiercely droning sandflies.

They dozed and mumbled to themselves.

They remained awake and tried to believe that somewhere on earth there was a place that was cool.

And then . . .

And then seven men holding automatic pistols came quietly into the room.

One of them remained at the door. The others spread out along the centre aisle between the two rows of bunks. They faced alternate ways, thus keeping every bunk under observation.

The more wakeful of the legionnaires jerked themselves into a sitting position. They gazed slack-mouthed at the guns.

The man at the door said: 'You will not be harmed if you do as I say. But . . . '

A couple of shots sounded from the ramparts. They were followed almost immediately by a choked-off scream.

The man continued: ' . . . but you may be shot if you attempt to disobey. Don't worry about what we are doing and why. You will know soon enough. Just obey orders. Your first order is to stand at the side of your beds, each of you with his hands on his head.'

There was no reaction — save for the creaking of bunks as the more somnolent roused themselves into consciousness.

And for the sudden angry buzzing of the sandflies who were jerked off their moist bodies.

'Do as I say. *Stand up!*'

The last two words were pitched at a near-scream. Twenty-two perplexed heads turned towards the door and studied the man who was threatening them. They saw a man who was much the same as the other travellers — for they were all much alike. They saw a large-faced, hard man. A man who was familiar with his Luger.

More than half of the legionnaires obeyed. They smiled sheepishly, as if wondering whether it was all some subtle and obscure joke.

The rest remained still — a few because of sheer lack of understanding, others because of gathering resentment.

That legionnaire on one of the middle bunks, for example . . .

He epitomized dawning hostility. It showed in his slate-blue eyes, in the compression of his slightly over-wide mouth. It was even reflected in the sudden tensing of his bare shoulders, where the flowing muscles suggested rhythmical speed rather than animal strength.

Legionnaire Keith Tragarth was English. Almost typically so, but not quite.

His blond colouring and pleasantly regular features fitted his island race. So did his faint West Country accent. Centuries before, Drake had been glad to hear that accent spoken around him on the decks of the little ships. So had Frobisher, Raleigh and Howe. Clive had been reassured to hear the burr of the Devon men among those who fought at Plassey. And Wolfe, when he scaled the Heights of Abraham.

Legionnaire Keith Tragarth symbolised some of the best characteristics of his country.

Yet . . .

There was something else about him. Something not quite in keeping. It could be sensed rather than observed.

Perhaps it was a slightly furtive air. A faint aspect of shame, such as a man feels when he shares a festering secret with his soul. Perhaps it was a tinge of only half-suppressed fear . . .

Keith said slowly: 'It would be a help if you'd let us know what the hell you're supposed to be doing.'

The man at the door understood the accented English. But he answered in French as he levelled his gun specifically at Keith.

'I will count to three. If you are not standing by then, I will kill you.'

There was a momentary pause.

'*One!*'

Keith glanced to the right hand side of his bunk. His Lebel stood there in its wall stand. It was within easy reach. But it was quite useless.

He would be shot down before he could lay a finger on it. And, in any case, it was unloaded. In accordance with standing orders, the magazine had been emptied when he last came off sentry duty and the cartridges had been restored to his leather pouch. All the others were in the same impotent position. A position in which, although they heavily outnumbered the men with Lugers, although they were technically armed, although they were the trained soldiers of a garrison, they were entirely helpless.

'*Two!*'

Keith felt the eyes of the other recumbent legionnaires upon him. They were looking to him for a lead. They would do what he did.

Keith got slowly off the bunk and placed his hands on his head.

He knew that he had no reasonable choice. Like any other sane man, he did not want to die. And he had no intention of dying stupidly and uselessly.

There was a stir of reluctant activity as the others followed suit.

There was a mumble of astounded fury, richly laced by profane oaths in many tongues.

They were ordered to march into the compound. The oaths increased in vehemence and volume.

But they marched.

Or rather they shambled, not looking like soldiers. They were a miserable handful of humiliated men who had been vanquished without a fight.

Lieutenant Andre D'Aran wanted to vomit.

He had to fight down the bitter liquid which gushed up from his rebellious stomach.

As he stood at the window and stared out at the compound he told himself: 'I've never seen men killed before . . . I'm inexperienced . . . only two years since I passed out of St. Maixen . . . never been in action . . . I didn't know that men could die so easily . . . like that Spaniard died . . . It's so simple, it's almost disgusting . . . and the Russian . . . he's still living . . . his legs are twitching . . . '

Gallast was directly behind him. It seemed that Gallast had heard the half-whispered phrases, for he said: 'You should not be so upset, lieutenant. Death is the coinage of a soldier's trade, is it not? And so is defeat. We all must suffer defeat sometimes.'

D'Aran did not attempt to answer. He continued to watch.

He watched the remaining sentries

form into a group in the centre of the compound.

But his eyes were dragged back to the twitching Russian.

He watched the rest of the garrison emerge from the building, escorted by more men with Lugers. With their hands on their heads they looked foolish.

But he had to steal another glance at the Russian.

He saw the Russian as a memorial to something. To human cruelty, perhaps. What was his name? Ah, *oui*, Vakasky. He had been a good soldier, had Vakasky, when he had not been serving in a punishment squad. He wore many medals, marking more than twenty years of campaigning. Vakasky had been in the Legion when he, D'Aran, had been in swaddling clothes. Now his medals were pressed into the dust. So was the red mess of his mouth. So this was how a soldier's life could end! Without dignity, without comfort. With only agony as a companion. Dogs died better deaths . . .

Gallast said: 'It is obviously the first time you have witnessed such things, lieutenant. I sympathise. But one gets used to them. Now I want you to sit again at your desk. I promised you a full explanation and you shall have it.'

D'Aran turned. He faced the Luger. That was all that seemed to matter about Gallast — his Luger. Not the man himself. He was nothing. It was his gun which made him important.

He took three faltering steps and sat down again in his chair.

Gallast sat, too. He poised himself easily on the corner of the desk amid the mass of papers. He was about to speak when one particular paper caught his eye. He picked it up, read it. It was the decoded message from the High Command.

'This,' Gallast said, when he had finished, 'shows that I am a very fortunate man. The transmission timing proves it came in less than half an hour ago. If we had been only a few minutes later in arriving at the fort you might not have allowed us in. We would still have seized the place, but it would have complicated matters. I fear our intelligence has been at fault — we did not think that this message would go out for at least another day.'

D'Aran's feeling of revulsion was fading. Curiosity was becoming predominant.

'Will you stop talking about things I cannot possibly understand? You have seized this outpost through a trick. Obviously you are not archaeologists. Equally obviously, you are soldiers. But who are you and why are you here?'

Gallast shrugged his broad shoulders. He waved the message.

'But you must have guessed that this is why we're here.'

'The — the bomb . . . '

'Exactly. Our precise nationality does not matter much, but let it suffice to say that we represent a government which is very curious about the forthcoming thermonuclear explosion. It is vital to us that we find out as much about it as possible.'

D'Aran swore softly.

'How can you hope to discover anything of use? Do you imagine you will get anywhere near the bomb before it is detonated?'

'We are near enough, lieutenant.'

'Near enough! It's to be exploded near the Sanna Oasis. That's thirty miles from here!'

'Quite so — but this place is conveniently located as an observation post.'

D'Aran drew a shaking hand across his damp forehead. He wondered again whether he was dealing with a madman.

'An observation post! *Tiens!* You've seen for yourself that we cannot remain here — it is much too close. Nothing can live in this fort when the explosion comes. The whole of Zone Zero is unsafe.'

'But we are not going to stay in the fort during the explosion.'

'Then how can you . . . ?'

'How can we observe the bomb? That will not be difficult. We have brought shock and heat-proof recording instruments with us. We will install them under the cover of your walls. Then we will leave them, retiring to a safe distance. When it is safe, we'll return to collect the instruments, which will tell our nuclear scientists most of what they want to know.'

D'Aran said tonelessly: 'How did you get into Algeria?'

'There was not much difficulty about that. When one is backed by all the resources of a powerful state, there is no particular problem about infiltrating into such a vast area as this.'

D'Aran had to admit to himself that this was true. Supported by a detailed organisation, there were at least a score of plausible routes by which twelve men could get secretly into the territory from Europe.

And despite the overwhelming horror of the situation, D'Aran found that pure curiosity was gradually overcoming all his other emotions.

He asked: 'You are not scientists. How can you install such instruments?'

'We don't intend to try. Professor Daak, of our nuclear research bureau, will arrive here at midday tomorrow for that purpose . . . he will arrive by air.'

'By air! *C'est impossible!* The range is

too far and the plane would be seen.'

Gallast gestured slightly with the gun.

'You are out of touch with modern developments, lieutenant. You ought to know that a long range bomber, carrying extra fuel tanks, can easily make the four thousand-mile return flight between central Europe and central Algeria. And it will not be seen, for it will fly most of the way at more than thirty thousand feet.'

'But . . . but why didn't you bring this — this Professor Daak with you?'

'Because he has to bring certain extra equipment with him which was too heavy to bring on pack mules. And I can see that another question is forming in your mind. You are wondering why all of us did not come here by air. A moment's reflection ought to provide the answer. You see, our only chance of seizing this fort lay in duplicity and surprise. We knew that it was a tiny and lonely place. We knew, also, that it was situated in a quiet area, therefore you were not likely to take precautionary measures against a handful of travellers who said they were looking for ancient remains. But if a large aeroplane had landed, it would have been different. You would immediately have been on the alert. As matters stand, our operation has worked very well. Professor Daak (a most talented and unusual man, I assure you) will arrive in comfort. And we will all leave for Europe in the plane, which will call back for us. We dare not keep the machine here in case it is seen by Arabs or damaged by the bomb. All the instruments will be buried after the vital data has been collected from them.'

There was a long and heavy pause. Then D'Aran moved a hand towards his tunic side pocket.

He said: 'Do you mind if I have a cigarette?'

'Do — but don't attempt anything stupid.'

D'Aran extracted a black enamelled case. His initials were on it in gold lettering. For a fraction of a second he recalled that Lucinne had given it to him not six months ago. She had pressed it into his hands and kissed his cheek at the same time, as if it atoned for her faithlessness . . .

But the digression was forgotten even before he put a cigarette between his lips. His brain had become a fevered tumult. He was watching Gallast under half lowered lids. D'Aran knew that he was not particularly big, and certainly not nearly as strong as Gallast. But . . .

But if he could overpower him temporarily. Just long enough to get an emergency call over on the radio set. Such a signal *might* be picked up first time, particularly since the powerful station at Sidi Bel Abbes had been using the wavelength less than an hour before. It was quite possible that one of the operators at Bel Abbes was maintaining a continuous listening watch on Fort Ney in case of queries arising out of the evacuation orders . . .

Oui, it was worth trying. Anything was better than this! And as he came to the decision, D'Aran was faintly surprised to note that he was not afraid. He was only tense with anticipatory excitement.

It was apparently as an afterthought that he said to Gallast: 'Do you smoke?' and offered his case. Gallast hesitated.

Then he took a cigarette. D'Aran produced a box of matches and struck one. Gallast leaned slightly forward to receive the light, his gun raised so that it was aimed at D'Aran's chest.

The burning match travelled towards the cigarette.

Then, at the last moment, it changed direction. The flame licked against Gallast's hairy gun hand. Gallast took in a swift, hissing breath of pain as he twitched the hand away. And D'Aran drove a fist into his face. In that transient period Gallast was an ideal target. He was off balance and on the corner of the desk. His gun was temporarily useless and he had no other defence. A right upper cut of only nominal accuracy and power would have put him on the floor, even if it did not knock him out.

But D'Aran was no pugilist. He hit while still sitting, instead of rising with the blow. And his knuckles landed on the bridge of Gallast's nose, where they had the minimum of effect. The result was that, although Gallast reeled off the table, he managed to keep his feet. He stumbled backwards and sideways, arms outstretched to maintain balance.

D'Aran jumped up. He remembered a brass paperweight on the desk. He grabbed it and threw it as Gallast was again levelling the gun at him.

There was no time to take careful aim. But this time he was fortunate. The heavy lump of metal struck Gallast on his right elbow. Gallast grunted under the shock and involuntarily opened his hand. The gun crashed to the stone floor.

Both dived for it together.

But D'Aran, because he was lighter and more nimble, got there first.

He landed with a breath-shaking jolt on his chest. His fingers closed round the Luger muzzle. A second later Gallast's heavy body dropped on top of him, across his shoulders.

D'Aran tried to twist free. It was impossible. The weight was crushing. He kicked in a futile way as he felt Gallast wriggle round. He knew what was going to happen. Gallast was about to link his fingers round his throat and throttle him.

He felt the fingers, thick and strong,

groping under his collar. He felt sudden pressure over the gullet. Then, suddenly, his head felt as if it was expanding under an intolerable internal pressure as the blood supply was cut off from his brain.

Instinct aided him — an instinctive recollection of a simple counter-move in unarmed combat.

He felt for Gallast's little fingers. His senses were fading fast as he grasped them and pulled outwards. But he had just enough strength to break the throttle hold. And as the pressure ceased his head seemed to clear miraculously. It was like coming to the surface after spending a long time swimming under water.

Somehow he managed to hold on to Gallast's weakest fingers as he suddenly arched his back. Now, because Gallast was himself leaning backwards in an effort to get free, D'Aran was able to throw him clear.

And as he did so there was a faint snapping sound from Gallast's right hand. The small bone there had broken before it had slipped from D'Aran's grip.

Gallast gave a grunt which turned into

a low groan. But D'Aran was scarcely aware of what had happened.

He had retrieved the Luger.

Holding it, he staggered to his feet, his breath coming in retching gasps.

Gallast was sitting upright. His hard-hewn face was distorted with pain. His close-cropped fair hair glistened with sweat.

D'Aran said jerkily: 'If you try to call out . . . I'll shoot you. Understand?'

There was no reply. No vocal reply. Only an expression of submissive hatred.

D'Aran backed towards the radio table.

Still watching Gallast, he fumbled for the main switch, locating it by touch. When it was pressed down he heard an oscillating whine emerge from the headphones. It was a strangely comforting sound. But he did not put the headphones on. This was no time for an awkward one-handed manoeuvre. His main concern was to get a message out. He would listen for a reply — if a reply came — after that.

Transferring the Luger to his left hand, he started to tap with his right. He gave the fort's brief recognition call twice. Then he immediately went into the message. It was brief. And there could be no question of coding it. He was not well enough versed in cipher to be able to code a message verbatim.

He tapped out: *Hostile forces seized fort to observe explosion.*

He hesitated, wondering whether to add anything to it. He decided not to do so. Those seven words were enough. Far better use whatever time was available in repeating the message.

His breathing was easier now and he felt calmer as he prepared to transmit again.

But at that moment a violent and fiercely echoing crash came from the doorway. At the same time D'Aran felt his gun hand become numb, useless. The Luger fell on to his lap, then slithered down his legs to the floor.

One of Gallast's men was standing there, a thin thread of smoke coming from the gas port of his pistol.

Vaguely, D'Aran heard someone shouting from outside. Then a clattering rush of feet.

The feet were still clattering, and getting louder, and louder, and louder, when he realised that the bare room was revolving round him.

Then there was blackness in the moment before he folded to the floor.

★ ★ ★

He was still on the floor. Gallast was standing over him, looking an evil mountain of a man. And for a time all D'Aran wanted to do, all he could do, was to stare upwards.

Then he became aware of two facts.

There was a dull pain in his left shoulder which centralised in a small area of clotting redness. It seemed that his wound was not too serious.

And a buzzing was coming from the radio. The same few Morse signs were coming over again and again. He concentrated. It was an effort, but he managed to follow the signal.

It was a call from Sidi Bel Abbes.

And it was saying: *We received only last word of your message. Word was*

'Explosion'. Please repeat at once.

D'Aran tried to match himself against another seeping wave of despair. And Gallast was smiling now.

'You heard, lieutenant?' Gallast asked.

'I did.'

'I am glad — it is as well that you fully understand your position.'

D'Aran groped for some means, however feeble, of upsetting this man's suave confidence. Eventually, he said: 'The High Command will be puzzled — they'll send out a patrol.'

'I think not, lieutenant. I myself will send back a suitable message, purporting to come from you. It will be an ordinary and harmless enquiry ending with the word 'Explosion'. It will satisfy them.'

He had been idly stroking his now bandaged finger.

Suddenly he bent down. With his uninjured hand he jerked D'Aran to a sitting position. He thrust his face close to that of the Frenchman. He said with a queer, calculated malevolence: 'I have yet another item of information for you. I intended to break it to you gently, for I am a tolerant man, but you have lost my sympathy . . . '

He broke off as D'Aran tried to shake himself free. It was a useless attempt. Gallast had a strong grip on his tunic.

'You can say nothing more that can interest me, Gallast — if that is your name.'

'It is my name, even though I introduced myself with the wrong title. I am Colonel Gallast, of . . . but that does not matter. Now listen to me, you young fool. Listen carefully. Have you thought of what we intend to do with you and your men during the explosion?'

D'Aran realised that he had not.

'I suppose you'll murder us.'

Gallast lowered his head momentarily in a movement which was half a nod, half a bow.

'Yes, we'll murder you. But it will be in the cause of scientific investigation.'

'Scientific . . . *tiens*, what do you mean?'

'I mean that you and all of your garrison will be trussed up like pigs, and left like that when the explosion is due.

58

That is Professor Daak's particular wish. He intends to use you all as human guinea pigs. In previous fission experiments, men have had to rely upon captive animals to observe the effects on living matter. This will be the first occasion in which human beings have been used. We will gain much additional information about the bomb when we return to examine your remains . . . '

4

The Bondage of Shame

A dismal streak of faint light percolated through the windows of the main bunk room. It played regretfully upon the huddled lines of men. Haggard men. Bewildered and frightened men. Men whose only solace was to know that the first night of painful captivity was almost over. They hoped that the ropes which held their wrists and ankles would now be removed — if only for a short time.

None of them had slept much. Sleep had been almost out of the question since their lieutenant had told them why the fort had been seized.

Told them, too, of the part that had been planned for them . . .

They were a normal cross-section of soldiers. There were fools among them. And those who were not so foolish. Cheats and liars were there. And they rubbed shoulders with men who observed simple standards of honour. There were a few bullies. But most possessed a crude type of gentility.

In fact, despite their varying nationalities, they were much the same as any other normal group of people on any other part of the Earth.

Except for one dominating emotion.

All of them were afraid. Very afraid. The dread of the future delved deep into their souls. But most of them managed to disguise the fact. Most conquered the moral paralysis.

Sergeant Vogel, for example.

Vogel had spent the night twisting on his bed because his dress cape — still on his shoulders when he had been seized — had formed into a hard ball beneath the small of his back. When he turned on to his stomach the material contrived to move with him. So he returned to the orthodox position. And there, as he shuffled, he thought.

Sergeant Vogel was an avid reader. He was the sort of person who consumes literature in the same way that a drunkard imbibes alcohol. He did so with fierce enthusiasm and absolutely no discrimination. It was not unusual for him to be seen reading a tattered American pulp magazine one day, and a complex work on international currency variations on the next. That Vogel did not properly understand much of what he read was of little importance to him, since he was unaware of the fact. He firmly believed that he understood everything he read, and he was happy in that belief.

He had brought a large supply of literature with him from Tala Baku. It was the harvest of many days spent at the market stalls there. He had secured half a dozen ancient editions of *Weirdly Horrible Yarns*, published in the American idiom and therefore to be construed with some difficulty by Vogel. He also possessed a copy of Einstein's *The Evolution of Physics*, in a Dutch translation. He had been looking forward keenly to studying this. Then there was a long, complete novel entitled *The Romance of Lottie Dene*, and Doctor Johnson's philosophical diatribe *Rasselas*.

By which examples, the catholic nature of Vogel's taste may be judged.

But it was none of these works which had been on his mind during the night.

It was a book he had read months earlier which arose in his memory as he twisted and turned.

The title was *A Treatise on the Elements of Atomic Power*. It contained many pages of advanced mathematical calculations which Vogel had studied laboriously and with an absolute lack of comprehension. But he clearly recalled some sections of the text. And particularly one paragraph dealing with the potentialities of the hydrogen bomb.

'The hydrogen bomb,' the author had explained, 'is an explosion resulting from the thermo-nuclear release of energy when hydrogen nuclei are condensed into helium nuclei.'

This had been impressively meaningless to Vogel — like the clash of tom-toms at a primitive tribal ceremony.

But the continuing sentence had been clear enough. It said:

'This explosion is similar to the

continuing reaction in the sun and other stars. On earth it can result from the triggering of the hydrogen bomb by an ordinary atom bomb.'

In other words, the explosion due near the Sanna Oasis would produce the heat of the sun in the immediate area!

Vogel understood the necessity for evacuating the whole of Zone Zero, save for the security troops, who would be under protective cover. He understood, too, all living matter left in Fort Ney would be baked alive in addition to being riddled with gamma rays.

As the daylight became stronger, Vogel came to a decision.

'I will kill myself before I let that happen to me,' he muttered.

Legionnaire Keith Tragarth lay on his side, watching the gathering light. He thought: 'It's going to be a hell of a way to die . . . '

And he wondered whether it would not have been better if he had been killed years ago, when he was a corporal in a British armoured regiment.

His mind roved back in time.

And as it did so, it revealed anew the festering shame which was always with him.

It was not a very unusual story. But, Keith told himself, it was a squalid one.

When, exactly, had he decided that he would ultimately desert from his regiment? Whenever Keith asked himself that question, he could not be sure of the answer.

Perhaps the decision came during the ghastly battle for Caen, soon after D-Day. During those days when the British and Canadians were engaging the entire weight of the German Panzer divisions, so that the Americans would be able to deploy on the right towards the vital port of Cherbourg.

He had been jittery all through the battle, and his tank crew had noticed it. But they had not said anything. They had even pretended not to know that he had mistaken a visual signal — and nearly landed the whole squadron into a minefield.

It had been the same months later, soon after they had crossed the Rhine. He had made more mistakes and only the quickness of a junior officer had saved them from disaster. A severe reprimand from the colonel had followed. Perhaps it was then that he decided to desert.

The colonel had not known (he could not have been expected to know) of the persistent sensation of tension which Keith had been experiencing. Of his inability to sleep, even when resting behind the lines. Of the times when — without any apparent reason — he broke into deep sweats. Of the desire to go to some quiet place and weep like a child . . .

In fact, although Keith himself had not known it, he was suffering all the symptoms of battle-fatigue. It was not unnatural, since he had been in almost continuous action since the breakthrough more than two years before, at Alamein.

Keith ran away when his armoured division was rolling towards its assembly area prior to a drive beyond Lubeck.

There had been nothing dramatic about it. He was not even in any particular danger at the time. He had simply taken advantage of a night-time refuelling stop to walk off.

He had done so because he could not face the coming battle. His nerves simply would not endure again the ghastly and evil music of death.

For weeks he walked westward, resting by day in woods and barns and eating only raw vegetables plucked from the land. Sometimes he saw motorised columns of Allied troops rumbling east — ever east. And he turned his face away in shame.

And all the while his soul craved only one thing — peace.

But he never found peace.

Not when (by describing himself as a refugee) he found farm work in the department of Loiret, in central France.

Not when he watched the peasants celebrating with wine and song the end of the war in Europe.

Always he was seeing the faces of the comrades he had deserted. Those ghost-like faces tortured him.

Which of them had died in the battle for Lubeck?

Which of them survived to see England again?

Was there always a strained and embarrassed silence whenever his name was mentioned?

Perhaps in some English inn one of his old comrades would say: 'Keith wasn't a bad chap — pity he was yellow . . . '

Or maybe someone who was less generous commented: 'Keith Tragarth never had any guts. I remember he was so scared once that he nearly took us into a minefield . . . '

He had not dared to return to England. Not even when the general amnesty for deserters was announced. He knew that if he did so the old and disgraceful story would be resurrected. It would reflect upon his family in their little village in Devon. And he himself would see the averted faces, the false courtesy. He would know what they were saying when he was out of earshot.

The war had been over for more than seven years when he decided to attempt an atonement. Something which would salve his raw conscience. He was working as a waiter in a cafe at Toulouse at the time. The big Foreign Legion recruiting depot at Marseilles was only three hundred miles away.

He bought a one-way rail ticket.

The Legion helped him. Basically, he found it much the same as the British army. In some respects the discipline was more severe, but in others it was comparatively lax. Certainly there was little of the fiendish bullying which popular but ill-informed opinion had led him to expect.

He found a new comradeship among the strange medley of nationalities. Men accepted him as another man — and no one enquired too closely about his past.

He had spent a few months fighting the rebels in Indo-China. And there he had been astonished and delighted to find that he no longer wanted to run in the face of danger. He had even managed to carry on for a full day with an undressed leg wound. It was that wound which had caused him to be invalided to a base hospital in North Africa — then to garrison duty at Fort Ney.

Yes, the Legion had helped. There had been times since he joined it when he almost forgot that once he had broken faith.

But the memory was never quite dead. It was always there. Always insidiously jabbing at him. Always sapping at his confidence.

He was a tragedy, was Legionnaire Keith Tragarth. He believed himself a coward, when in fact he had been too brave. His only crime was that once, years ago, he had carried on beyond the point of nervous endurance — and paid the penalty with a complete moral collapse . . .

And as the morning light grew stronger, Keith twisted to look at the floor of the bunk room in Fort Ney.

There, on the smooth stone, was the huddled figure of Lieutenant D'Aran.

D'Aran had been bound and thrown into the room with the rest of them.

Keith saw the wound on the officer's shoulder. It was unbandaged — a black mess of congealed blood over a ripped tunic.

He said: 'Are you all right, *mon officier?*' But D'Aran did not answer. He did not hear the question. He was temporarily unaware of the pain in his shoulder; unconcerned by the plight of the garrison.

D'Aran was thinking about fifty thousand francs. And about Lucinne . . .

The Brazilian consul-general at Tala Baku was giving a reception when a friendly staff major came up to D'Aran and said: 'You've been watching that woman Lucinne Ranoir a lot this evening. Take my advice, and don't bother much about her. She can only bring trouble.'

D'Aran had felt indignant. It was an unwanted piece of interference. But a junior lieutenant, if he is wise, does not show indignation to a field officer. So he had merely said: 'She's very beautiful. One can hardly avoid looking at her.'

The major had laughed as he put a hand on D'Aran's shoulder.

'So long as you only look, you'll come to no harm,' he had said. Then he had moved away across the ballroom.

D'Aran wished the major had not

departed so quickly. He wanted to ask questions.

Why should such a lovely creature as Madame Ranoir imply trouble? It was preposterous! He watched her as she whirled in a waltz. *Dieu!* Such raven-haired gaiety, such electrifying charm. True, she was a widow and no doubt had known deep personal tragedy. But, in D'Aran's eyes, that only served to magnify her attraction.

He forgot the major's warning. Before the reception was over he had contrived an introduction. And five minutes before the orchestra played the Brazilian anthem he had asked her to dine with him. She accepted without any pretence of hesitation. She was a forthright woman, was Lucinne.

They met the following evening and went to Baku's only fashionable restaurant — a pleasantly discreet place with palm-lined balconies on the edge of the desert.

Many other Legion officers were there, but mostly of senior rank. It was seldom that a lowly lieutenant could afford such a place, and D'Aran was shocked to find that his bill deprived him of nearly half a month's pay. But it was worth it! *Ah, oui!* A thousand times it was worth it, to be in the company of such a happy, such a fascinating, such a glorious creature.

Lucinne talked a lot that night in her rich and racy voice, emphasising each sentence with vivid gestures.

She told him that she was a Parisienne. It was in Paris that she had studied art — but without much success.

'In that I had no talent,' she said with gentle lowering of long lashes over green-grey eyes. And D'Aran had felt a new surge of excitement. There was a wealth of suggestion in that simple admission.

They returned to the restaurant later in the week. And Lucinne told him about her husband. He had saved her from penury as an artist by his offer of marriage.

But, Lucinne told him, it had not been a happy marriage. He was a Bolivian in the consular corps and much older than she. That was how she came to Tala Baku.

And it had been in Baku that he died suddenly a year earlier.

Why had she not returned to France?

Because she liked Baku — liked the vibrant life of the Legion base.

This peculiarity of taste was beyond D'Aran's comprehension. To him — as to all soldiers — Tala Baku was a dust-blown apology for a town. Much the same as all military bases, except that it was infernally hot by day and bitingly cold at night. A place in which there were far too many men and lamentably few women . . .

But D'Aran did not worry much about this strange choice. It was enough that Lucinne *was* there.

Before he could meet her for the third time D'Aran had to borrow money.

He was not a habitual borrower. His normal tastes were simple enough. Therefore one of his fellow subalterns was a trifle surprised when D'Aran asked for ten thousand francs until the end of the month. But the money was borrowed without difficulty.

At the end of that particular evening

D'Aran tried to explain to Lucinne.

'I'm afraid we won't be able to come out again for a couple of weeks,' he said, blushing deeply. 'You see . . . I'm a bit short of cash.'

Lucinne regarded him levelly. Her joyous effervescence had diminished. But D'Aran did not notice.

'You have no private income?' she asked.

'No — I'm afraid I haven't.'

'But surely — most officers don't rely entirely on their pay.'

'This one does . . . ' He hesitated, then added with a rush: 'I'm not one of the fortunate ones. My parents died when I was young and they were not wealthy.'

'Then how could you afford to become an officer? The St. Cyr military academy is expensive, is it not?'

'I did not go to St. Cyr. Most Legion commissions are granted from St. Maixent and I won a government grant to pay for my training there.'

She stubbed out a cigarette thoughtfully.

'You must be very clever,' she said.

'Non, I don't think so. It was just that I had always wanted to serve France in the Legion, and to win a state scholarship was the only way. A man can get almost anything if he really wants it.'

'Including a woman?'

The question was so sublimely sudden that he was momentarily confused. Before he could evolve an answer, she was adding: 'I like you, Andre. I like spending the evenings with you, for you are a welcome change from the fat and old men. But I did not know you were poor. It is not fair to you that I should spend your money at such a place as this, is it? I think it is better that we do not meet again.'

He felt as if she had slapped his face. Yet he was not annoyed with her. But, for the first time in his life, he resented his poverty. And he was ashamed of it.

And he was going to lose her!

It was unthinkable.

He looked across the table at the sensuous suggestion of her shapely body, at the tempestuous beauty of her features, and he knew that he would not let her go

76

away. He could not do so. She had taken possession of him. She had become the dominant part of him.

He lied. He had never before been a liar.

He told her: 'It's not as serious as all that. I have money saved. Why shouldn't I spend it on you?'

Lucinne brightened immediately. Her old animation returned, as if at a flick of a switch.

She put out a hand and touched the tips of his fingers.

'I think I like you very much, Andre,' she said . . .

After leaving her that night, he went into the card room in the officers' mess. He played until five in the morning.

And when he left the table he owed nearly forty thousand francs.

'I'll settle later in the day,' he promised his creditors. And settle he must.

But how?

His total debts were now fifty thousand francs. His assets were nil. Even his entire month's pay — when it arrived — would not be enough. It had all happened within twelve hours.

And what about Lucinne? He had promised to meet her again that night under the wild notion that he would be lucky at the table.

There was only one solution. Since his gambling debts *must* be paid immediately, and since he *must* see Lucinne, he would have to borrow again, on a long-term basis. The lieutenant who had advanced the original ten thousand would almost certainly help — for he was of a wealthy family.

But that lieutenant was not to be found. He had departed on a few days' leave.

D'Aran felt dizzy when he established the appalling fact. He felt a great wave of panic seize his vitals. It would be bad enough to face the social disgrace of not meeting gambling dues. But to have to admit to Lucinne that he was a cheap liar, too . . .

That was impossible.

Then he remembered the mess funds.

Those funds, raised by voluntary subscription, were used to obtain occasional extra comforts for the mess. And he, D'Aran, as one of the most junior officers, had been placed in nominal charge of them. So far as D'Aran could remember, there was about seventy thousand francs in cash in the orderly room safe. If would be easy to take fifty thousand of it — then replace it when he had raised a loan. And he could foresee no possibility of detection, for the audit was not due for a fortnight and there was no likelihood of a call on the money.

He hated himself for the decision. He hated himself as he waited for the orderly room to be temporarily empty.

And he hated himself as he unlocked the safe and removed the notes.

But he was driven by a fathomless compulsion.

That afternoon he paid the card players. Then he went into town to pick up Lucinne at the small hotel where she stayed.

He was approaching the entrance when he saw her leaving. She was on the arm of a colonel of the *Tringlots*. They got into a Legion staff car and drove away.

He stood very still in that street, with

the throng of Arabs and soldiers pressing about him.

Then he groped in his breast pocket for the photograph which Lucinne had given him of herself.

He tore it into precise fragments. He watched them fall to the ground.

And then, because an infatuated man knows no logic, he knelt down and retrieved the pieces.

★ ★ ★

He had just finished pasting the torn shreds together when the adjutant came into his room.

'I'm sorry about this,' the adjutant said, 'but you've been posted to Fort Ney. I know it isn't your turn, but there's been some trouble with the rota. You'll leave with your column in the morning.'

Several seconds passed before D'Aran could answer. Then he said: 'Must it be me?'

The adjutant looked curiously at his white and working face.

'Of course it must be you. No other

subaltern is available and we can't very well post a captain to a miserable little place like Fort Ney, can we? But why are you so bothered about it? I know it is a wretched place, but it's only for three months . . . '

D'Aran was wondering when his friend would return from leave. Wondering when he would be able to borrow money to replace that which he had taken from the safe. He was not likely to be back before the end of the week. By that time it would be too late. He, D'Aran, would be well on his way to that damnable outpost. And in a couple of weeks the theft would be discovered.

Then . . .

They would wait for his return under the normal trooping arrangements. And when he was back at Tala Baku he would be called before a General Officer's Enquiry. After that he would be arrested.

A court martial after that. Then a ceremonial parade at which the badges of rank would be ripped off. After that, a prison sentence . . .

★ ★ ★

81

... As he mused, D'Aran was only vaguely aware of the morning light. Scarcely sensible of his shoulder wound. Nothing mattered now. Only the past was real — and it had the reality of a shadow.

There had been no substance in anything since that day he had marched out of Tala Baku, knowing he had left behind a crime which would surely be unearthed.

And now, as well as disgracing his name because of a woman, he had smeared it through military incompetence. D'Aran thought as he lay bound on the floor: 'I'm inept. If it weren't so serious I'd be a public joke. Secrets of the new bomb will be revealed to our enemies because I was duped. And our very corpses will help the enemy in their work . . . '

As if from far off, he heard the words being repeated from the bunk at his side:

'Are you all right, *mon officier?*'

It was a call to the present, to the immediate and ghastly chaos which was Fort Ney.

He eased from his side to his back and looked up at Legionnaire Keith Tragarth.

'*Merci, legionnaire*. My wound is not serious. It is not that which is worrying me.'

Keith said: 'Do you . . . do you think there is anything we can do?'

D'Aran considered before replying. 'This is the last day of June,' he said. 'We have eight days before the explosion.'

'A lot can happen in eight days.'

'*Oui*, a lot can happen — or nothing at all.' As soon as he had uttered the words D'Aran regretted them. His was the duty of encouraging his men, not of damping down their hopes. So he added quickly: 'But somehow we *must* get a message out. It is not just a matter of our own lives, nor even of preserving the secrets of the nuclear explosion.'

There was a sudden atmosphere of tenseness in the bunk room. All the other legionnaires were awake and listening to D'Aran now. Realising this, D'Aran raised his voice slightly.

'It is the Arabs who matter, too,' he said. 'My orders were to evacuate all of them from this command area by midnight, July the fourth. If that is not done, they will die in their hundreds when the bomb is detonated. It will be awful . . . and it will be a crime for which all humanity will hold France responsible.'

Keith said: 'That means we really have only four days.'

D'Aran grunted.

Sergeant Vogel, who was still half-considering his reading on nuclear fission, said from the other end of the room: 'There would be no survivors, *mon officier*. The heat alone would kill everyone within forty miles if they were not under cover.'

No one thought of questioning this statement. Vogel's mental storehouse of miscellaneous knowledge was well known.

Keith said: 'But the evacuation will go to plan in the other command areas of Zone Zero. Surely the Arabs in this area will hear of what's going to happen and clear out?'

'That's not likely,' D'Aran answered. 'This command area must be the most isolated in the whole of Zone Zero. There's not much chance of the Arabs in it hearing anything about the coming explosion unless we can tell them.'

There was a bleak silence. It was broken as Vogel contorted over the hardness of his cape. Then Vogel said diffidently: '*Mon officier* . . . the Sanna Oasis is only about twenty-five miles from here. There must be many scientists and technicians out there at this moment assembling the bomb. I think there will be some Arab labour, too, for I have read that such a weapon would be exploded from a high steel platform.'

'That's probably true, sergeant.'

'And there will be a heavy Legion guard there, also.'

'*Oui*, obviously.'

'Then, *mon officier*, as we are the nearest military post, will they not try to get in touch with us?'

D'Aran considered. Then he said: 'I think not. There's no reason why they should want to communicate with us so long as they don't suspect that anything is wrong. And I think the High Command signal would have mentioned the fact if

85

any contact had been planned.' There was a faint but clearly audible sigh of disappointment from some of the legionnaires.

Keith said: 'There must be an Arab habitation at the Sanna Oasis — and we are supposed to remove them. When we don't turn up the Legion commander at Sanna must guess that something has happened.'

There was a stir of interest at the logical conclusion. But again D'Aran had to give a pessimistic reply.

'I wish you were right,' he said. 'But I happen to know about the Sanna Oasis. It is not an oasis at all — it is no more than a name. There are wells there, but they dried up ages ago, so there is no Arab habitation anywhere near the place. So you see — we will not be expected to clear the population out of Sanna, for there *is* no population!'

Another silence.

Then a babble of voices.

'So we're cut off!'

'Just got to spend a week here!'

'Trussed like hens!'

'Waiting to be murdered by the bomb!'

Sergeant Vogel restored order. The Dutchman forgot the discomfort of his cape. He ceased to think about the book on atomic power. He inhaled air into his considerable lungs and screamed a single word.

'*Silence!*'

It was like a steam whistle tearing asunder the tortured air. It produced an absolute, cloistered quiet.

And it was then that a key turned in the door.

Gallast stood in the threshold, two others immediately behind him. Despite his bulk, Gallast could suggest the attribute of cultivated courtesy. He was suggesting it now. He gazed around him with a hurt and bemused expression.

'Did I hear signs of panic?' he enquired of no one in particular. There was no answer. He continued: 'I don't want to make your period of waiting more unpleasant than it need be, for above all else I am a soldier and I want to observe the civilised rules of war . . . so far as that is possible.'

D'Aran twisted himself into a sitting posture against the wall.

'*Sacre bleu!* Is this part of the civilised rules of war! Is it civilised for soldiers to pose as civilians and seize an army post which was offering them hospitality? Is it civilised to plan for human beings such a fate as you have waiting for us? You do not know what the word means . . . you are a barbarian and you belong to a creed which embraces barbarism!'

Gallast was watching D'Aran calmly. Ostensibly, he seemed unmoved. But a faint twitch of pain momentarily etched into his face, and it may not have been caused by the injured finger which he was stroking.

'You speak wildly, lieutenant,' he said. 'But you are very young and it is understandable. You think we are responsible for organised savagery against you. But isn't that taking a rather limited view? Think again about that bomb which is to be tested . . . think of its destructive power. What would it mean if it were used against my people and we had no power of retaliation? Is it not our duty to do all in our power to discover all we can about it? Of course it is. And if the only way we can do that is through methods of ruthless audacity, can you blame us for using them? Would France, would any country, refrain from such measures if the whole of their existence were in the balance? Certainly not. But understand this. I personally get no pleasure out of contemplating your fate. Neither does it worry me. It's simply a manoeuvre in an undeclared war. That you and your legionnaires are to die is a mere chance of war!'

A shiver seemed to spread through the cheerless room. There was no answer from any of the bound men.

Gallast continued in less precise tones: 'But you'll be wondering how you are to spend the remaining week of your lives. Obviously you cannot remain bound hand and foot for the entire period. So this is what I intend — you will be freed during the daylight hours only. In that time you will assist in the installation of the observation instruments. All the time you will, of course, be closely guarded. But . . . but if any of you has any idea of escape, or of damaging the instruments, let me say this — the man responsible will *not* be harmed!'

The pronouncement came like a stabbing electric shock. D'Aran said faintly: 'Did I hear you correctly? Did you say you will *not* harm . . . '

'That is what you heard, lieutenant. If a man tries to escape — and escape will be quite impossible — he will simply be brought back. He will not be harmed in any way. The same applies if he attempts any sabotage. *But . . . one of his comrades will immediately be selected at random and executed . . .* '

D'Aran had regained some composure, but he had to struggle to retain it.

Eventually he said: 'That's a new twist to a devilish technique.'

Gallast nodded.

'Quite so. It is my experience that men will always risk throwing their own lives away in what they conceive to be a good cause. But they hesitate to endanger the lives of their friends.'

He glanced at his wrist watch, then added: 'It is now nearly nine o'clock. The ropes will be removed. You will have food. Then you will wait until the plane arrives.'

5

Out of the Sky

A vulture hovered over Fort Ney, wings flapping like the feathers of a battered fan. It cocked a cruel head at the tiny walls, at the ridiculously small compound building. Then it squawked its amusement — as they were all said to squawk — and wheeled away towards more serious affairs.

But its progress was disturbed.

A black dot, getting steadily larger, was coming down upon it from the vivid blue of the midday sky. As it formed into a definite shape of wings and body and snarling sound, the vulture turned in its course and sought refuge among some distant rocks.

Within the four-engine bomber Professor Daak nursed a violent headache.

He sat amidships and in confused isolation. A single — and not too comfortable — chair had been installed for him. And around it was a closely packed and secured miscellany of wooden crates. The professor occasionally took a hand away from his throbbing head to regard the crates with distaste. They suggested several days of hard and complex work. And, at the moment, he did not feel like work. He wanted nothing so much as to feel his feet on mother earth, then go to sleep in a comfortable bed.

In short, the professor was not used to air travel.

He had felt ill ever since taking off many, many hours before from a European airport.

Twice he had stumbled forward to the crew's compartment with a request that they descend from the sub-stratosphere. The air pressure system was not in order, he declared. His head was bursting. But the crew showed lamentably little sympathy. After pointing out that they had received precise orders as to their flying height and route, they ignored his alternating threats and supplications.

Therefore it was with relief that Professor Daak felt the plane suddenly tilt down in a steep dive. As he fumbled to fasten his safety belt he muttered to himself words of consolation.

'We must be there,' he said. 'When I have rested I will feel better. Then I will start work . . . '

★   ★   ★

The legionnaires were assembled in the compound. Six of Gallast's men — now armed with Lebels as well as Lugers — were watching them from the ramparts. The legionnaires were staring at the huge plane as it touched down more than half a mile away, then disappeared from sight as it stopped within thirty yards of the walls.

The silence seemed unnatural as the engines were switched off.

Then the gates — those puny gates — were opened. Gallast walked briskly out and towards the massive hulk of the machine.

He reached it as the side door opened

and a steel ladder was let down on to the sand. A man in a grey uniform and a heavily braided cap descended. He was followed by two others similarly dressed. They saluted. Gallast, although in mufti, returned the salutes.

Gallast said: 'I congratulate you — your timing is excellent. Has he taken the trip well?'

The pilot gestured towards the plane.

'He has not. He says he is ill. But it's nothing — just the changes in atmospheric pressure.'

'And the equipment?'

'All here and unharmed.'

'That is good. Now perhaps I'd better see the professor.'

They started to move towards the plane. But at that moment Professor Daak appeared at the top of the ladder. He made a strange spectacle.

He was a small, stocky man, with an enormous paunch which strained against his quite unsuitable blue serge suit. Although he was well past middle age, he had the sort of pink, unlined oval face which suggests perpetual astonishment.

At the moment his face was swathed in an unhealthy sweat so that it looked as if it had been coated with a transparent varnish. Whisps of grey hair protruded forwards from under his formal black hat. He was breathing heavily and painfully.

Professor Daak, emeritus lecturer in nuclear physics, looked ridiculous as well as ill.

He swayed at the top rung of the ladder and attempted to descend the wrong way round. The co-pilot and the wireless operator went to his assistance.

When he was safely on the sand Gallast shook his clammy hand. He said formal words of greeting, then added: 'All has developed according to orders. The garrison has been captured and until the day comes they will be put to work. They are ready to unload the equipment.'

Daak groped for a pair of pince-nez spectacles, clipped them on his angular nose. 'I must rest,' he gasped. Gallast smiled.

'Certainly, professor. You have had a trying journey. But first you must supervise the unloading. Only you know how these delicate instruments must be handled. Without your assistance they may be damaged.'

Daak breathed yet more heavily. Despite his distress, he injected some force into his words.

'But I must lie down first. My heart — it is not strong. My head — it aches. This heat — it is like an inferno. I am not used to such heat. I am not used to anything here. Give me a little time.'

The pilot shuffled uneasily as he met Gallast's eye. He tapped a finger on his watch. Gallast took the cue.

'We cannot wait, professor. You must know the orders — the plane has to be unloaded immediately and return without delay. Once the plane has gone everything here will appear normal to any passing Arab caravans. But if they see it here, they will talk. And such talk may reach French ears.'

'But just an hour . . . '

'Not even an hour. That is final. In all other matters I will be under your orders, professor. But on questions of security you must obey me.'

Daak looked as if he was going to protest again. But he did not. Even as he opened his arms to make a gesture the co-pilot took advantage of his position to remove his thick jacket.

Gallast gave a thin smile of approval.

'Now you will be cooler,' he said. 'The work will not take long. I'll call out the legionnaires.'

* * *

Under the threat of Lugers and Lebels, the garrison moved out of the fort and towards the plane.

And there was something strange about the way they moved.

They no longer shambled. Nor did they walk in everyday fashion.

They marched.

Without D'Aran or Vogel giving any order, they had formed themselves into files of three. They carried themselves stiff and upright. Their heads were held high. They kept parade ground step.

Though they did not fully realise it themselves, this was a return to their innate sense of discipline and to a pride in their calling. It was one way of showing that they were not yet cowed. Not finally defeated.

In fact, the garrison were recovering fast from the first paralysing shocks. They no longer lived entirely with fear.

They had become men again.

And as such, they had become dangerous.

It was slavery — serf-like toil in an oven. The crates varied only in the vastness of their weight. Not all were large, but often the smaller ones seemed the heaviest. They had to be carefully lowered out of the plane with ropes, then dragged slowly over the sluggish sand to the fort.

The legionnaires were divided into two sections — a smaller party of six (including D'Aran and Keith Tragarth) working inside the plane. The rest, Vogel among them, handled the crates when they reached the ground.

After hesitating about his best location, Professor Daak supervised from inside the bomber. There, at least, he was sheltered from the direct rays of the sun. And, sitting in his passenger seat, he recovered some of his vigour.

His breathing became more controlled. His orders became more precise — and more exasperating.

It was the manner in which he delivered those orders. Like a chemist repeating the results of a clinical test. He did not speak as if he was dealing with flesh and blood. His attitude towards the legionnaires was that of a master to trained animals. He possessed a high-pitched voice, almost like a woman's, which seemed oddly appropriate coming from his smoothly pink countenance. His words were delivered in fluent French . . .

' . . . knot the rope tighter! Tighter, I said!'

' . . . don't bump that crate! I won't tell you again!'

' . . . now down with it! Down!'

The work was almost finished, after two fiendish hours, when the tragedy of Legionnaire Paffal occurred.

Keith was the cause of it. The accidental cause.

One of the last crates for unloading was very small. And, for once, it was not particularly heavy. Keith lifted it unaided and moved towards the door of the plane. There, he intended to place it near the edge, rope it, and lower it to the waiting legionnaires.

A short length of thick rope for this purpose had been left on the floor, near the door.

It was by pure chance that Keith stumbled on it. As he attempted to regain balance a foot caught in the coil. He lurched against the angle of the open door and the steel frame jabbed his hands.

The crate slipped free and fell ten feet to the sand. A hysterical scream came from Daak, then a flow of vituperation.

Gallast, who had been standing near the nose of the plane with the crew came swiftly over. He mopped his sweating face before looking up at Keith.

'This is unfortunate,' Gallast said.

Keith was rubbing his hands. He said curtly: 'It was an accident.'

'Accident! You tried to make it look like

one, but I am not a fool. It was deliberate
. . . and you may recall my warning about
any attempt to damage the instruments.'

Keith remembered. He held up his raw
hands. Then he pointed to the offending
rope.

'You can see for yourself! I tripped
and . . . '

'Nonsense! You deliberately stumbled.
You deliberately hurt your hands. And
then you threw down the crate.'

Keith glared down at Gallast. But his
indignation was heavily tempered with
anxiety.

'I tell you I did nothing of the sort!
Anyway, what the hell are you worrying
about? It fell on soft sand, didn't it? It
doesn't look as if anything is broken.'

Gallast regarded the undamaged crate
thoughtfully.

'I won't know about that until the
professor has made an examination.'

Professor Daak had risen stertorously
from his chair. He stood beside Keith,
waving an accusing finger at him.

He screeched: 'I was watching! I saw it
all. He threw it out of the plane!'

Keith turned to face the paunchy and vicious little man.

'You're a damned liar!'

'Quiet! I will not have you speak to me so!'

Keith instinctively bunched his throbbing fists. He felt a strong desire to use them.

'If you weren't an old man,' he announced slowly and loudly, 'I'd take you apart.'

Professor Daak was no hero. And he was not content to rely upon his senility for protection. He retreated into the plane. Then Gallast spoke again.

'Everyone will get out of the bomber,' he rapped. 'I am satisfied with Professor Daak's statement. There is no need for further debate.'

Three guards with Lugers ushered them down the ladder. On further orders the other legionnaires ceased work and joined them. There was an atmosphere of morbid tension.

Gallast said: 'I made it clear that if there was any nonsense one man would be selected at random and executed — an innocent man. You can scarcely have forgotten. We will proceed with that unpleasant business without delay — I want to get the plane in the air as soon as possible.'

He spoke with casual indifference, as though explaining a minor hitch in army manoeuvres.

D'Aran pushed forward. His prematurely lined face was now more deeply etched than ever.

'You can't be such a maniac! I am ready to state on my honour that it was an accident — I saw it better than Daak.'

Gallast shook his head.

'I am sorry that I cannot accept the word of an officer — but there it is.'

'So you are going to pick out an innocent man and murder him!'

'I did not use the term murder. Execute is the more accurate description.'

Keith took a pace forward so that he was standing next to D'Aran. Some compulsion made him say: 'If you are determined on this, you might as well kill me. I dropped the crate.'

He felt them all looking at him. And,

strangely, he felt a deep and genuine hope that Gallast would accept. It would be an atonement . . .

But again Gallast shook his head.

'That is impossible. It is most necessary that the innocent should suffer if we are to avoid further trouble. The only question is who . . . '

His eyes travelled down the line of legionnaires. They returned and rested upon a small and tubby figure in the middle of the file.

Legionnaire Paffal . . .

Paffal was a Greek. He was justly proud of the fact. But there was nothing about his appearance or demeanour to suggest the ancient and modern glories of his race.

In his sweat-sodden shirt and baggy trousers he looked as if he had been moulded to shape in a barrel. Neither heat, not hard physical work, nor a frugal diet could remove his rolls of fat.

And he was a nervous little man, was Legionnaire Paffal. Not merely at this moment, but always. He was one of those unfortunate men who are forever anxious to please, but never quite succeed in doing so. In fact, if there was a wrong way of doing anything, Paffal would be sure to find it — despite his efforts to the contrary.

When loading a rifle he would contrive to jam the cartridges across the magazine spring. When on parade he would forget his number in the file. When detailed to scrub out a barrack room he would overturn the bucket of water on a legionnaire's only tunic.

Yet no one — not even the long-suffering Sergeant Vogel — could get really annoyed with Paffal. For Paffal tried so hard. And beneath his perpetual state of nervous flux there was a warm heart and cheerful nature. It was to Paffal that Gallast pointed. 'It will be you,' Gallast said. 'Walk away from us — two of my men will shoot you as you do so. You'll know nothing about it.'

A faint hiss of deeply drawn breaths spread down the file. It was followed by an ugly muttering.

D'Aran's face was contorted, his eyes wild.

'This is satanic! Listen to me . . . *I'll* have the bullet in the back. I'm the commanding officer here, so my life ought to satisfy you more than his!'

Gallast ignored the suggestion. He pointed again at Paffal.

'Do as I say,' he said briskly. 'You'll gain nothing by standing there for we can quite well shoot you from the front. But it will be better for you if you don't know the precise moment.'

Paffal's greasy round face looked as if it was being massaged by invisible fingers. His eyes were glazed. He tried to speak. No sound emerged.

It was then that the legionnaires moved — moved simultaneously.

They formed a shield of bodies round Paffal. They were not inspired by any discernible leadership. There was no suggestion of a word of command. It just happened. It was the sort of mass reaction which seizes men who have been pushed too far . . .

In one moment Paffal was visible in the centre of the file. In the next, he had disappeared. And the file had reformed itself into a closely packed mass.

After a moment of bewildered inaction, the guards raised their pistols and rifles. Then they looked doubtfully at Gallast.

Gallast remained very still. Almost unconcerned. But when he spoke his tones had a strained, echoing quality.

He said: 'If you do not move, you will be shot — all of you.'

They did not move. They stared back at Gallast. 'This is your last chance. In a few seconds I will order my men to fire.'

Absolute stillness.

It was as if the earth had ceased to spin in the heavens. As if nothing existed upon a torrid planet save this group of men standing outside a tiny military outpost.

It was uncanny. And like all uncanny things it could not endure for long. Either the rattle of firearms had to end it — or some action from among the legionnaires themselves.

It came from among the legionnaires.

From Paffal.

He pushed through the huddle of his comrades, his head bent low. When he emerged he had lost his *kepi* and the sun reflected off his shining bald scalp.

He made a nervous gesture. Then he said to Gallast: 'I am ready.'

Keith made a dart to him and grabbed his shoulder. But Paffal shook him off.

'I am ready,' he repeated. His voice had a firmness which had never been heard before. There was a strangely decisive air about him.

For a moment Gallast seemed confused. Then he said: 'I don't recognise your accent, fat one. What's your nationality?'

'I am a Greek.'

'Indeed . . . you surprise me. What is there about Greeks which makes them so willing to die?'

'I am afraid to die. But I would be more afraid if I saw my comrades dying because of me.'

Gallast nodded.

'You confirm my reasoning. But you also puzzle me. I know nothing about Greece which leads me to believe that its people are capable of such courage.'

'Then you truly know nothing about

Greece. My people have fought oppressors for thousands of years. They fought them just a little time ago when they broke the hearts of the Italian armies who tried to invade the land . . . I am not a brave man. Sometimes I think I am a very stupid and useless sort of man. But I can try to be worthy of my people, who have never been cowed by bullies such as you, for freedom . . . oh, but you would not understand!'

'I may not agree — but I will understand. Continue.'

'I was only going to say that freedom was born in Greece. But you can't know what freedom means!'

Gallast sniffed. It was almost an obscene sound.

'But I do know! Freedom is the privilege of serving the state with blind loyalty, for the state gives all and to the state we owe all. But . . . but as a soldier I respect you. I would be prepared to let you live . . . '

He paused and there was an eager hopeful stir among the legionnaires. It was frozen still as Gallast continued:

' . . . but I never rescind an order such as this. It would be an unforgivable weakness. March away from us . . . Greek!'

Paffal took a half step forward, then stopped. He looked confused.

'My cap,' he said. 'I've lost it. It would not look well if I died without wearing my cap. May I have it, please?'

The *kepi* was near Keith's feet. He picked it up and handed it to Paffal. He could not meet Paffal's eyes.

Carefully, Paffal adjusted it over his hairless head. But he was typical at the last. He failed to notice that at one side the chin strap had fallen away from the button. He had a length of thin black leather trailing past his left ear.

He walked away from them — a little unsteadily, but with no slackening of pace.

The legionnaires turned away as a couple of Luger shots rang out.

6

According To Plan

At Sidi Bel Abbes . . .

A cooling fan whirred discreetly over General Jonot's head. The sound blended with the hum of traffic in the street outside. The hot air was tainted with petrol fumes and the indefinite odour of the nearby Arab market.

The general was glancing at the reports on Zone Zero.

It was a leisurely process.

He would pick up a signal sheet from a small pile on the right of his desk. After a brief pause, he would initial it. Then he would transfer it to a growing pile at his left elbow. Occasionally the general would put a casual question to his deputy chief of staff, who sat opposite.

As, for example, when he came to the sheet headed *Fort Ney Area Command*.

General Jonot was about to initial it

when he paused, pen in contact with the paper. His brow became furrowed. He said: 'I see that we received a message from Fort Ney at 15.07 hours yesterday.'

His deputy nodded. 'I believe we did.'

'But only the last word could be identified!'

'That is so. The wireless room requested a repeat. It was received some twenty minutes later.'

General Jonot concentrated heavily upon the report sheet. Then he said: 'And when it arrived it was quite a trivial query. But it *might* have been important — and there was all this delay in making contact. It's not good enough . . . I have come to a decision . . . ' Jonot paused weightily. His deputy waited without much interest.

Then Jonot added: 'As soon as things are back to normal after the explosion we will have new wireless equipment installed in Fort Ney. Even a wretched little place like that must possess good communications.'

★　★　★

At the Sanna Oasis . . .

For centuries it had been a place of blistering desolation. Then the desolation gave way to seeming chaos. Men arrived. They came in massive transport planes and in huge track-laying lorries. They brought with them a weird conglomeration of materials. The Arab labourers among them built temporary huts which served as offices and living quarters. The soldiers circled the place with wire and minefields. And in the midst of it all a mast-like steel structure went up. Armoured electric cables — which had been fed from a point fifty miles due south — were installed at the top of the mast.

And now the evacuation was starting.

The Arabs went first, packed in the lorries.

The less senior technicians were following by plane.

For only seven days were left. And before six of them had passed Sanna would be deserted again.

Except for the protective ring of minefields, the wire, the flimsy huts.

And except for that stark steel mast which would become molten and vaporise when the thermo-nuclear bomb exploded on top of it.

★   ★   ★

At Tala Baku.

The colonel flipped through the Standing Orders Diary and said to the adjutant: 'I see the mess funds are due for audit at any time now. Let me see . . . who's in charge?'

'It was that fellow D'Aran.'

'D'Aran? Ah, *oui!* You posted him to Fort Ney, didn't you?'

'Yes. And for the time being I'm holding the safe key, *mon* colonel. 'I'll hand it to the auditor when he arrives.'

'Quite . . . you know, now I come to think of it, D'Aran seemed unusually depressed when he set off for Fort Ney. I happened to notice him on the parade ground. Still, I suppose the prospect of three months in that place would distress anybody.'

'He'll have plenty to occupy his mind, what with that infernal bomb going off.

It'll do him a lot of good, *mon* colonel.'

'A lot of good? I don't understand.'

'Well . . . he was heading for trouble, you know.'

'Trouble! He always seemed to me to be a reliable young man. No money, not much background, but efficient.'

'He'd been seen about with a woman. That Lucinne Ranoir creature. Beautiful — *oui*. But dangerous for one so young.'

The colonel removed his reading glasses and chuckled.

'Such women are only safe in mature and experienced arms — such as our own! Eh?'

'Certainly, *mon* colonel. I did not want to see him make a fool of himself — that's why I selected him for Fort Ney. He'll be well away from her. He'll be able to forget . . . '

At Fort Ney . . .

Keith strained instinctively against the ropes which had been newly tied for that night. He glared from his bunk at the similarly trussed figures around him.

'Why didn't we rush them?' he shouted.

Someone said: 'You talk like a fool. We

116

would have been killed.'

'We're going to be killed anyway, aren't we? We're going to be melted alive by that blasted explosion! Then we're going to be dissected by that fiend Daak, just so he'll know exactly what happened to us!'

D'Aran had found a spare bunk near Keith's. He twisted on it and said: 'Our duty is to remain alive as long as possible. While we live there is always a chance that we might be able to get a message out, so . . .'

'It's a slim chance,' Keith interrupted. 'The radio is the only way and Gallast and Daak have taken over that room. So what remains? I'll tell you — nothing!'

'Nothing would have remained for us if we had rushed the guards this afternoon,' D'Aran said logically.

The Dutch inflections of Sergeant Vogel boomed through the gathering gloom.

'*Mon officier*, I do not think they would have killed *all* of us. Some of us would have been overpowered — but allowed to live.'

'Indeed! Why?'

'Because the professor wants some of us to die from the effects of the bomb, *mon officier*.'

There was a brief silence while the sensible but macabre point was digested. It was broken by a nervous neighing from one of the horses which had been tethered in the compound.

A Czech, who could blaspheme fluently in six languages besides his own, demonstrated his verbal skill. Then he added: 'Those animals are getting tired of being kept out there. They'll make a lot of noise tonight. We'll get no sleep.'

There was a general groan at the reminder.

Then a legionnaire said: 'They'll be using those horses to get away before the bomb . . . '

' . . . And to get back to look at the remains.'

' . . . Then the plane comes again to collect them.'

' . . . So maybe the horses have a right to be miserable! *They're* going to work hellish hard, then they're going to be left to die!'

' . . . Like us!'

The staccato discussion went on, broken by an occasional uneasy laugh. But Keith did not join in. He was not even listening. He was thinking.

The horses . . .

If they could be killed, or even maimed . . .

Gallast depended on those horses, Keith suddenly realised. Without them, he would be unable to get away from the fort to take cover in the foothills.

Or would he?

Damn! Of course he would. He and his men were soldiers, too. They were tough. They could march if they had to, just as it had been planned that the garrison would march.

No — the idea was useless. It would have no more than a nuisance value.

But wait!

Professor Daak!

What about him? He was a sick man. They'd all heard him bleating about the heat and his heart. And he was old. *He* would never be able to march a single mile. And Gallast couldn't leave him. Daak was the key to their entire operation. He was the only scientist among them. And, of course, the spare horse had been brought to carry him . . .

Keith turned to D'Aran.

'Listen, *mon officier*,' he whispered urgently, 'I have a plan . . . '

D'Aran listened while discussions about other things went on around them. When he had finished D'Aran said levelly: 'It is a good plan, legionnaire, but it has one or two bad faults.'

'What are they?'

'It pre-supposes that at least one of us will be able to approach the horses. How are we going to do that?'

'There must be a way!'

'Perhaps — but what is it? We are bound hand and foot at night and there is a guard outside this door. By day their guns are always pointing at us.'

'We could make a rush for the horses.'

'*Tiens!* Another of your rushes! But suppose that your rush succeeds — what then? How are we to kill them? Do we choke them with our bare hands?'

Keith fought down a mounting indignation.

'Maybe we could lame them.'

'Lame them! Again I ask — how? A kick on a fetlock would not achieve much, legionnaire . . . except that the horse would kick back!'

There was a touch of good-humoured mockery in D'Aran's tones. Keith realised that his points were utterly logical. And that served only to make his disappointment the keener. He felt a perverse fury both with himself and his officer.

But his fury died as D'Arari suddenly said: 'But you have the germ of an idea! I think I can see possibilities . . . there are possibilities! We will have one chance in a thousand. We will need steady nerves and great patience. God in his heaven will have to protect us if we are to succeed. But we *may* succeed in cheating those swine if we follow my plan. And you legionnaires may escape with your lives . . .'

The last sentence spurred Keith to a quick interruption.

'How about *your* life? You speak as if you're not interested in your own future!'

It was almost dark now. Keith saw D'Aran only as a dim shadow. But he

121

sensed a stiffening of the officer's muscles.

And when D'Aran answered, his voice was harsh.

'Perhaps you are right, legionnaire,' he said. 'Perhaps you are right . . . '

Then he added briskly: 'The explosion is due at 15.00 hours on July 8th, which is just under seven days from now. But we must wait at least five days before putting my plan into operation . . . you see what I meant by steady nerves and patience? But if also means that we will have plenty of time to think of improvements! Now listen to me. Listen very carefully . . . '

PART TWO

(JULY 6TH–8TH)

1

Survey Report

Gallast directed a critical glance at a prostrate Professor Daak.

'You ought to be getting used to the heat,' he said.

Daak shuffled and grunted. He lay on an additional bunk which had been squeezed into D'Aran's room. He raised a sodden handkerchief in a trembling hand and dabbed sweat off his bare chest. Then, breathing noisily, he turned his astonished-looking countenance towards Gallast.

'I've told you before — it's my heart. I wish someone else could have come out here in my place. But then, there was no one with the knowledge.'

'You worry too much about yourself. Try using more will-power. Remember — you have an arduous day in front of you tomorrow. When the wretched legionnaires have been trussed up, we start riding for the safety of the foothills.'

Daak moaned at the prospect.

'By the way,' Gallast asked, 'can you sit a horse?'

'Perhaps. Perhaps not. It is many years since I tried.'

'Then you'll have to cling on as best you can. My schedule has been worked out to the minute and we won't have much time to spare. We leave here at two o'clock in the afternoon — that gives us just one day and one hour in which to cover the thirty miles to the foothills and dig protective trenches. In the ordinary way, there'd be ample time, but we must take supplies for several days on the pack mules, and mules will not hurry.'

A quiver of anxiety passed over Daak's pink and seamless face.

'Those trenches . . . they must be very deep and dug in a special way or our lungs will be blown inside out by blast, even if we do not die of burns.'

Gallast shrugged.

'That will be done — and we'll have the benefit of your expert advice.'

'But it will take many hours, even with twelve men. Could we not leave earlier? Why delay so long?'

'You want the legionnaires to be alive right up to the moment of the explosion, don't you?'

'But of course! If I am to know the precise effects of thermo-nuclear radiations on living tissue I must . . . '

Gallast cut in with an angry gesture.

'Then as a man of science you ought to know that they cannot last much longer than twenty-four hours without water and in the full heat of this sun. Don't forget — when we leave them they must be bound so they can't move an inch.'

Daak licked a pair of shapeless lips. The eyes behind his pince-nez suddenly flickered with academic interest.

'That is quite so. Forgive me, I was forgetting. And they must be placed in the exact spots I mentioned — half of them in the compound so that I can gauge the protective value of the walls, the rest just outside the south of the fort, where they will receive the full thermo-nuclear radiation.'

Gallast looked thoughtful. He said slowly: 'You know, Daak, I don't like you! You can talk with complete indifference about the fate of the garrison — not that I blame you for that. I am indifferent, too. But you are a coward when it comes to your own safety. As a soldier, I have a natural antipathy towards cowards.'

'You are insulting me! I, Daak, have . . . '

'I know! You are our foremost scientific brain. I don't deny it. But that's your trouble, Daak. You're all brain and no back-bone . . . but enough of this. I have a very important signal to send to the gentlemen on the Legion High Command. I must satisfy them that all is well . . . '

He sat at the radio table.

D'Aran's code book was lying among the assortment of valves and wires. Gallast worked with it for a full half-hour, checking and rechecking his message before switching on the set and picking up the earphones.

He tapped out the Fort Ney recognition signal, cursing the aged apparatus as he did so.

128

At last, after a long delay, a series of powerful long and short stabs rang in his ears. He made a brisk consultation with the code book.

The reception signal from Sidi Bel Abbes. Gallast braced himself. Then he transmitted the message.

From officer commanding Fort Ney. To secretary, High Command. All Arab populations now removed from area. Am evacuating garrison at 22.00 hours this day, as ordered.

He had scarcely finished when a return signal came from Sidi Bel Abbes. Gallast grabbed a pencil and took down the Morse. Then he transcribed it from the cipher key.

Please repeat from word 'garrison'. Last part of message not received clearly.

Gallast referred to his original coding and sent out the repetition.

There followed twenty minutes of

silence, save for the static from the earphones.

Then, after the usual preliminaries,

Sidi Bel Abbes said: *Explosion will take place as planned at exactly 15.00 hours, July 8. Follow previously issued safety instructions exactly. Bon chance.*

Gallast was breathing almost as heavily as Daak as he switched off. But he was smiling.

'At 22.00 hours tonight,' he said, 'I will destroy this radio set. There may be a test signal from Sidi Bel Abbes after that time to see if the place has been evacuated. They must be convinced that it is so. There must be no chance whatever of their picking up an answer.'

Daak said: 'Who would do that? You're the only one who can work the set?'

'I know that. But some fool might come in here and switch on. If that happened, the High Command station could get an answering beam. I insist on absolute safety.'

But Daak made no comment. He had

closed his eyes behind his pince-nez and was rapidly falling into a heavy doze.

Gallast put on his out-moded pith helmet and went into the glaring heat of the compound. It had changed vastly in the past few days. Beneath the south ramparts more than a score of curiously designed instruments had been assembled under Daak's supervision. Some of them were linked to powerful high-tension batteries. All were enclosed in thick metal cases which had been cemented into the ground. The legionnaires were providing additional protection by filling sandbags and placing them round the base of the instruments.

In a sense, Gallast had been relieved by the way the garrison had worked. Even after the example of Legionnaire Paffal, he had expected to have to deal with other rebellious incidents. But there had been none. The garrison had done as they were told. Sullenly, of course. But competently. They had not even answered the screeching vituperations of Daak.

Which, perhaps, was odd . . . Gallast had an uneasy feeling that they would try something soon. Time was running out, and he could scarcely expect nearly thirty tough soldiers to accept their ghastly and humiliating fate without some show of resistance.

Still, he was ready for it, Gallast told himself. His men would know how to handle them.

He approached Lieutenant D'Aran who, because his shoulder had not yet healed, was engaged in the comparatively light work of knotting the tops of the sandbags. There was, he decided, no reason for refusing D'Aran the final details. Gallast had a precise sense of fairness.

'You know the date, lieutenant?'

D'Aran straightened. He seemed to have become thinner in the recent days. Those premature lines had deepened at the corners of his mouth. There was a sense of strain about him. Like a spring waiting to be released. He nodded at Gallast, but did not speak.

'It is today that you were due to quit the fort. I have just had a radio exchange with your High Command and I've told

132

them that you are planning to leave.'

D'Aran showed a faint flash of expectancy. Gallast detected it. He said: 'No — there's no cause for hope there, lieutenant. The High Command did not suspect that anything is amiss. I took the greatest care. I studied copies of previous messages so as to get the correct style — though it is not very different from our own. And, of course, I used your invaluable cipher book.'

'It's very interesting. But why are you telling me this?'

'Because soldiers about to die are entitled to the last relevant details, even though they don't always get them. It only remains to tell you that we will not leave the fort until two o'clock tomorrow afternoon. Your own evacuation schedule was based on the assumption that you would be marching. We can afford to linger a little longer because we will travel on horseback.'

It may have been to cover a dangerous show of emotion that D'Aran said: 'It will be the end of a dirty piece of work . . . *monsieur*.'

The use of the civilian form of address was a calculated affront.

Gallast tensed.

'I do you the courtesy of addressing you by your rank. Please do the same for me! I am *Colonel* Gallast.'

D'Aran smiled. Then, with studied deliberation, he turned his back and continued work on the sandbags.

When Gallast had gone, D'Aran beckoned to Keith. As Keith was ostensibly preparing to drag a laced sandbag away, D'Aran whispered: 'They leave tomorrow afternoon! For us, it is tomorrow morning — or never!'

★ ★ ★

'Speaking in broad terms,' General Jonot boomed, 'I would say that we have fulfilled the trust placed in us. I have just finished examining the final survey reports from Zone Zero and I find them satisfying. There is no indication of activity by hostile agents. And, I am delighted to say, there has been remarkably little trouble with the Arabs . . . '

He glanced round the group of operational staff officers until he detected the elderly and faded colonel. Jonot directed an accusing glare in his direction.

'You, colonel, will be particularly interested in this. I recall that when we met a fortnight ago you foresaw much trouble with the native populations.'

'I still foresee it, *mon generale*. The enforced evacuation must have caused a great deal of ill-will.'

He waved his copy of the survey report and added: 'There has been some trouble with the Arabs in each command area of the Zone, according to this . . . '

'Except in the Fort Ney area.' The colonel gave a puzzled nod.

'*Oui*, I see that Fort Ney sent a signal this afternoon reporting that the evacuation has gone to plan. They make no mention of meeting any hostility. I'll admit I'm surprised. I can see no reason why the Fort Ney area should differ from the others.'

Jonot fumbled in his despatch case. He produced and consulted the trooping schedule.

'Fort Ney,' he announced with some drama, 'is commanded by a Lieutenant D'Aran. That name may be worth remembering, gentlemen. D'Aran is obviously a highly competent officer. I will congratulate him personally at the earliest opportunity. It has always been my policy to encourage those who carry out their orders with imagination and ability ... that brief, succinct message we received from him this afternoon reflects a clear mind working with smooth efficiency. One or two senior officers here might study Lieutenant D'Aran's methods with advantage, for I have always said ... '

The general was enjoying himself.

And his operational staff suffered in respectful silence.

2

One Gun . . .

D'Aran did not sleep that night.

He writhed against his bonds like a man in a fever. His mind was a hot tumult. He tried to calculate the diminishing hours to dawn. But he had lost all sense of time. There was only blackness. Only the night was real. The night and the fear which stalked within him.

Supposing they failed?

But they were almost certain to fail! It was not really a plan they were going to put into operation. It was a mad tilt at the wheel of chance. A gambler's last throw against odds of a thousand to one.

It all turned on at least one gun and an extra clip of ammunition. One was as important as the other. A Luger alone, holding a mere ten rounds, would be next to useless. Those additional cartridges were essential.

But would they get either?

It would be a divine act of providence if they managed to snatch the pistol from the guard. But surely the Divinity would not intervene twice!

Non, it would fail. And some would die with slugs in their bellies. Just as the Russian had died. But it would be worthwhile. In fact, those who were shot would be lucky. Better to go that way than to be trussed like cattle and await the explosion.

And why should he, D'Aran, worry? He had nothing to live for.

That safe in the orderly room . . . it would surely be opened by now. And he would be branded a thief. A cheap little upstart. A disgrace to the uniform of France.

Lucinne . . .

Dieu! He hadn't thought of her for days! Yet she had possessed him once; held his whole body and mind in serfdom. And now . . . now he could think of her with cold indifference. He could see her for what she was. Well, what was she?

A tramp!

Oui, a tramp in rich clothes! And Lieutenant D'Aran had been a piece of garbage she had picked up, then tossed aside!

He started to laugh. A low-pitched but hysterical laugh. It stopped when Legionnaire Keith Tragarth whispered: 'You all right, *mon officier?*'

So the Englishman was awake, too!

Legionnaire Tragarth would die tomorrow — or was it today? He would either die at dawn when their bonds were unfastened, or at 15.00 hours in the afternoon . . .

But Tragarth would die honourably. Like a man. Tragarth did not know the agonising humiliation of hating oneself.

Ah *oui*, lucky Legionnaire Keith Tragarth!

* * *

Damn you, you're yellow! Keith told himself.

You always were yellow. Didn't you shake your pants off when the creeping barrage started at Alamein? Oh yes; you got through all right! You managed to fight it down and you got a Mention in Despatches. Plus a nice spray of laurel leaves to stick on your medal ribbons. But God, no one knew how scared you'd been!

The same in Italy.

Before the first bloody attack on Monte Casino you got down on your knees and prayed when no one was looking. Yes, prayed! Pleaded for a little guts!

And hadn't you been glad when you got a gun-shot wound in your leg!

It meant safety in a base hospital while better men were being blown to bits.

You were glad, too, when you were sent back to England. On leaves between assault training you were able to walk amid the peace of Devon again. And hope that perhaps the invasion of Europe would never come. But it came. And you, Keith Tragarth, were quaking in one of the first tank landing craft. You fought your way up the beach in a blank daze.

You were in a daze all the way across France.

Then you quit! You turned and ran!

'I'm a gutless swine,' Keith whispered. 'I *deserve* to be haunted by the men I betrayed in Germany. The men who fought and died while I was skulking away . . . '

He heard a laugh.

It came from D'Aran's bunk. Keith collected himself and murmured: 'You all right, *mon officier?*'

D'Aran became quiet after muttering something.

And Keith thought: 'So he can make a joke of it all! He'll die tomorrow, but he'll die like a man. He won't hate himself.

'Ah, lucky Lieutenant D'Aran . . . '

★　★　★

Full daylight.

But no heat yet in the sun. It directed pale shafts of light on the bunks and on the bound men.

There was a strange lack of movement among those legionnaires. Almost as if they were corpses.

And there was but one sound — the

141

droning of the sandflies as they darted from man to man getting their morning fill of salty sweat. It was a good day for the flies. No bodies were contorted to throw them off. They bit and they sucked at leisure. For the legionnaires scarcely noticed their presence.

Then, from beyond the locked door, footfalls. They echoed dimly as they approached. Each separate impact between boot and stone seemed to say, '*soon, soon, soon . . .*'

It was a signal for a relaxing of the tension. Simultaneously, all the legionnaires eased against their constricting ropes. There was an automatic flexing of muscles. A simultaneous licking of dry lips. The sandflies lofted angrily to the ceiling. The footfalls had almost reached the door.

Soon, soon, soon . . .

They stopped. A clink of keys. A rasping insertion into an old and massive lock. The turning of the mechanism, which was a mere mass of mechanical agony.

And the door was open.

Six guards entered, all holding Lugers. They paused on the threshold, making a swift preliminary inspection. Satisfied, two of them advanced to untie the bonds so that the legionnaires could eat, drink, and attend to the other needs of nature. The four others remained just inside the door.

It was a long tedious process, that freeing of the ropes, for they were always knotted with skill. The two guards progressed along at either side of the room, taking nearly two minutes to each man.

They did not appear to notice that as each legionnaire was released he spent more time than usual in massaging life back to his painful limbs. Nor did they attach much importance to the fact that there was less talk than normal. Men facing death are not usually loquacious,

After nearly half an hour, the final rope was lifted away from the last wrist and ankle.

And one of the guards jerked his thumb towards the door.

By now that was a familiar signal. It

meant that Sergeant Vogel and Legionnaire Keith Tragarth were to go through the normal process of collecting the morning rations. When they returned — and not a moment before — the others would be allowed out two at a time to visit the adjacent wash-house.

The guard, who was pock-marked, said to Keith and Vogel: 'You'll have coffee today instead of water. And there's a double issue of pemmican biscuits.'

Keith tried to appear casual as he asked: 'Why the sudden charity?'

'It's no charity,' the guard assured him with a humourless smile. 'We're building up your strength. We want all of you to be alive when the explosion comes.'

Keith did not answer. The pock-marked guard followed them as they moved out of the room. The five other guards stood against the wall, Lugers still held ready.

Like everything else in Fort Ney, the cookhouse was a dismally inadequate structure. It was a small square place situated between the bunk room and the officer's quarters.

The water storage tank lay under the floor. Being fed by a natural artesian spring, it maintained a constant depth of rather more than nine feet. Access to it was gained by lifting one of the large flagstones.

A small oil stove stood against one wall and above it hung a miscellany of antiquated cast-iron cooking utensils. The rest of the space was taken up by deep shelves on which various dried foods were stored, several sacks of flour and chicory-laden coffee, and a small wood table.

Two tall pitchers, in which water for immediate use was kept, stood in one corner.

The guard spat on the floor. Then, posting himself just inside the open door, he said: 'We want coffee also. Make plenty of it. And make it fast.'

Keith thought: 'The coffee's a bit of luck. It gives us extra time . . . they'll think we're making it . . . '

While Vogel went to one of the coffee sacks, Keith picked up the stone pitchers. As was usual at that hour, one was empty and the other nearly so.

Keith crossed to the well flagstone. He prised up the rings in the centre. With an effort — for the stone was heavy — he lifted it clear.

Black water was revealed beneath.

Meantime Vogel had emptied coffee beans into a pan. He now turned his attention to one of the shelves. He took down a large lead-plated case. This contained the pemmican biscuits.

There was an air of resigned efficiency about their actions.

Until Vogel dropped the case.

It was not an abrupt drop. Rather did he let it slither out of his hands, so that one corner hit the floor without any considerable noise. The other corner fell on the stiff toe-cap of his left boot.

But Vogel gave out a gasping moan. He lifted his left foot and held it between his hands. Face contorted, he hopped round the floor.

The guard looked at him without sympathy.

'Fool! Pick it up and get on with your work.'

But Vogel did not do so. He leaned

against the wall directly behind where Keith was kneeling and continued to moan softly.

'Be quiet! You're not hurt!'

Vogel continued to ignore the guard. He had the appearance of a man battling with a severe injury.

The guard hesitated. For a moment it seemed as if he was going to put his head into the short corridor and call for one of the others. But instead he decided to investigate himself. Holding his pistol at waist level he took a pace towards Vogel.

'Let me see that foot.'

He was glaring down at the allegedly damaged limb.

Vogel detached a hand from it to make a shaking gesture.

'I've — I've broken a bone . . . I'm sure I've broken a bone. That box . . . it fell across my ankle.'

By now the guard was half convinced.

'Then get back to your bunk. You have one consolation — it won't hurt you for long!'

He started for the door.

He intended to move backwards — so

as to keep Vogel and Keith in sight. But before a man can progress in that fashion he has to be certain that his path is clear. Even as he took the first short step the guard felt compelled to glance quickly round.

It was precisely the moment for which Vogel had been waiting.

The Dutchman stopped nursing his foot. Suddenly he kicked with it — a vicious kick. The boot slapped into the crotch between the guard's legs.

A violent blow in that area has an unusual temporary effect. It induces complete temporary paralysis of the entire body, including the vocal chords. But there is no immediate loss of consciousness. The recipient is aware of each figment of appalling agony without being able to give so much as a low moan.

For perhaps a couple of seconds the guard stood completely still, absolutely rigid. His eye-balls had rolled upward so that only the whites and the lower rim of each cornea showed. There was a barely detectable twitching of his cheeks.

This condition was due to last for less than half a minute. Then life would return to his motor nerves. He would let out a piercing scream — if he had the opportunity. He was not given the opportunity.

Vogel took hold of the limp gun hand. He inserted a finger behind the trigger before removing the weapon from the man's grip. By this means he prevented any possibility of it being accidentally fired.

He glanced at the gun belt. It was a military type, with an ammunition pouch at the right hand side. But, as they had foreseen, there would not be time to remove this. Already the guard was producing a series of faint grunts. Any one of them might be heard by the others, less than five yards away.

Keith whispered: 'Hurry! What are you waiting for?'

But the phlegmatic Vogel took his own time. He gripped the guard round the shoulders and waist. He half lifted, half pushed him backwards.

Like all the others, the guard was

powerfully built and heavy. Even Vogel's considerable strength would not have been enough to prevent him hitting the floor with a loud bump, if Keith's kneeling body had not been in the way.

As it was, he fell silently across Keith's back.

Keith squirmed free of the burden. Then, with the guard stretched near the edge of the water tank, Vogel carefully reversed the Luger, so that he was holding the barrel. He took careful aim, then tapped the man's forehead with the heavy butt. It was not a hard blow — a hard blow might have been noisy. But it was sufficient to stop the grunting by producing complete unconsciousness.

Both Keith and Vogel were sweating hard. But they worked as if doing a drill.

Vogel pocketed two clips of spare ammunition.

Keith took up the pitchers, filled them to the brim. Then he concealed them behind the oil stove.

They froze still as they heard a cough. It came from the bunk room. Then a mumble of guttural voices. The guards were talking. Maybe they were becoming impatient.

Now the worst moment of all.

For a moment they stood on either side of the prostrate body, looking at each other. Keith had to fight against a sickening revulsion. But they gained strength from each other's presence.

They bent down. Slowly they dragged the guard so that his head hung over the water tank. Then they pushed.

The senseless man slid face first into the deep, dark water. He did so slowly, and there was scarcely a splash.

As the water closed over him, a circle of air bubbles rose and plopped on the surface. Then there was nothing — nothing to suggest that a man was dying nine feet below.

Keith moved swiftly to a shelf. His moment of revulsion had passed. He felt a great exhilaration as he took down two large hemp bags of salt. These, too, were lowered gently into the tank. Then, very carefully, they replaced the flagstone.

They braced themselves. Vogel patted his tunic pocket to assure himself that the

Luger and ammunition clips were there. Keith whispered: 'Remember — we're puzzled. We're annoyed . . . '

Vogel nodded.

Keith leading, they moved into the short corridor. To their left they saw the open door of the bunk room. They saw part of the back of one of the guards. And beyond him the legionnaires, who were standing in small groups, or sitting on the edges of their beds. D'Aran was nearest the door. He looked straight at Keith. Keith nodded.

Deliberately, D'Aran called: 'Why are you standing there? *Tiens*, don't we get any coffee?'

'No water,' Keith called back, and he was surprised by the calmness of his voice. 'We can't get it out of the tank because those damned pitchers have disappeared.'

A couple of guards appeared in the doorway. Their pistols were held ominously ready as they surveyed Keith and Vogel.

One of them rapped: 'Where's Sarle?'

Sarle, it seemed, was the man in the tank.

Keith shrugged.

'He went to look for the pitchers.'

An expression of baffled wonder crossed the guards' faces. It was quickly replaced by one of acute suspicion.

'Move back three paces and stand against the wall!'

Keith and Vogel obeyed the order. The two guards advanced to the cook house. One kept his pistol aimed at them while the other looked inside. He emerged after a quick glance.

'Not here,' he said. Then added: 'The fool! Gallast will have his skin for this — leaving two prisoners!'

They exchanged oaths. Then suspicion reappeared to take the place of indignation. 'Where are the pitchers?' Keith made a helpless gesture.

'I don't know. Perhaps Sarle will know. He ought to have found them by now.'

'Did he say where he was going to look?'

'He said something about seeing if Gallast . . . '

'*Colonel* Gallast!'

' . . . if Colonel Gallast had taken them.

He thought perhaps the professor had been ill in the night.'

'And drink eight or nine gallons of water!'

'They wouldn't be full, but there would be a few drops in each.'

Keith realised that he had made a mistake in introducing the reference to Gallast. It would have been more convincing if he had stuck to the original plan, which was to plead absolute ignorance.

But Vogel came to his aid. Vogel said vehemently: 'Must we spend our time talking about what you swine may have done? We want those jugs! We want them now! And we want them because we are thirsty! If you can't find them we'll look ourselves!'

Vogel was showing unsuspected theatrical gifts. He was shaking with anger when he finished. The two guards looked doubtful. They glanced towards the bunk room where the legionnaires had moved nearer the door, despite the pistols. They were straining with apparent curiosity.

It was then that a slight commotion

occurred in the-bunk room.

It was centred around Legionnaire Batini, an Italian who possessed a luxurious black beard.

Batini was gesticulating lavishly as he poured forth a torrent of garbled explanation.

'I had the duty to do last night,' he said. 'Thus I put them behind . . . they are better behind for they are smart are they not? They will be behind the stove now where I put them when I cleaned the cook house . . . why was I not asked? Am I a fool? Am I not right . . . ?'

He was interrupted by a crash of carefully simulated anger from his comrades. Then D'Aran called out: 'You'll find the pitchers behind the oil stove. It seems Batini put them there when he was cleaning the place.'

Keith laughed. Then turning to the couple of guards he said: 'I think we're all too thirsty to wait for coffee.'

He went to the stove and pulled out the pitchers.

'They're here all right,' he said clearly. 'But it's a damned awful place to put

them. You'd think they'd been hid-
den . . . '

Vogel took one from him. Together they
carried the water into the bunk room.
They deposited the pitchers a few feet
from the door where three guards stood.
The two others had departed to look for
the missing Sarle.

Keith watched while the legionnaires
drank.

Then casually, Vogel said: 'We must eat,
too. I'll get the biscuits.' He moved out of
the room.

Probably because their numbers had
been reduced, the guards hesitated about
having him followed. It was a fatal
hesitation.

Immediately Vogel was beyond the
threshold he stopped. He swivelled on his
heel. He re-entered the room holding his
Luger.

There did not seem to be any interval
between his reappearance and a shattering crash of fire from several pistols.

Vogel, being a Dutchman, was a realist.
By the same token he was a brave man.
Therefore he almost certainly knew that

he would die. Tactically, his position was quite impossible.

The three guards were standing against the wall — two on the left side of the door, the other on the right.

The first shot came from Vogel. He aimed at the single man at his right side. The heavy slug lifted off the top of his skull as if it was on a hinge.

But he had not time to turn completely round to face the others. Nor had the legionnaires time to rush to his assistance. Four bullets entered Vogel's large body before the garrison, headed by Keith, closed with the men who had fired them.

But some men do not easily say farewell to life. Some men die hard. Vogel was one of them.

A hot slug had passed at an oblique angle through his chest, carrying fragments of the second and third ribs with it when it dropped on the floor behind him.

And — as a strange quirk — the ankle of his left foot was smashed.

But he reeled against the door. He leaned his great weight against it so that it slammed shut. He was on his knees when he groped feebly for the heavy bolt. His last action was to push it into the socket.

Then, shattered face against the woodwork, he died.

The legionnaires . . .

It had been easier for them. Much easier than they had expected. The two remaining guards had had no chance to confront them after shooting Vogel. They crashed to the floor under a mass of cursing, clawing, kicking men.

Keith got one of the pistols after a quick wrench at a wrist. But he was knocked down by the impetus of the legionnaires behind him. He found himself kneeling on top of the guard, who was already semi-conscious as wild boots thudded against his cropped skull. One kick, intended for the guard, sent a rasp of pain up Keith's thigh. He wanted desperately to get out of that avenging mass, but he could not.

But presently D'Aran's voice cut through the confusion.

'*Gare a vous!*'

The command was theoretically ludicrous at such a time. But any such theory discounted the effect of prolonged military training under inflexible discipline.

The legionnaires drew away from the two guards — both now disarmed and severely injured. They came to an approximate position of attention, all dishevelled and breathing heavily.

D'Aran had gained the other gun. He gestured with it ferociously.

'*Sacre!* Must you behave like a mob? Our real work has scarcely begun. Have you forgotten the horses?'

Then he turned and ran to the window at the far end of the room, Keith at his side.

It was a narrow window and (as was the habit in Legion forts) protected by widely spaced iron bars. They stood on a bunk to peer through.

The horses were there. Thirteen of them, plus the mules. They were tethered to individual wood stakes which had been driven into the ground. They were less than fifteen yards away. Slightly beyond and to the left were the tents where Gallast's men slept.

D'Aran checked the ejection action of

his pistol. Then he turned a tense face to Keith.

'I feel more sympathy for the horses than I do for the two-legged swine,' he panted. 'But this has got to be done . . . don't miss . . . '

They aimed carefully through the bars. And a second afterwards the air was again filled by the harsh explosions of Luger cartridges. It was a cruel, satanic spectacle.

The first four slugs were well directed. Each hit an animal in the upper part of the head. They were dead before they fell sideways to the ground. But by this time the others had taken panic. They reared on their hind legs as though performing in a circus ring and whinnied like sobbing children.

An expert marksman using a rifle under ideal shooting conditions might have been able to dispose of them humanely. But it was beyond the powers of two men, holding unfamiliar pistols, and aiming between iron bars. Several shots missed completely. Most of the others hit where they would kill but slowly. These fatally wounded horses lay beside the more fortunate dead, thrashing their hooves.

But two of them escaped entirely.

Both were powerful mares which were tethered further away than the others. As they reared they dragged the stakes out of the baked ground.

Then they bucked wildly for a moment before stampeding towards the tents.

Keith managed to aim a shot at one of them, but it churned up the sand far ahead. Then they had passed the tents and were out of sight, although the thudding of their hooves as they circled the compound could still be heard.

D'Aran said: 'Wait! They may be back.' They waited for a full minute. But suddenly the thudding ceased and there was a distant cry of voices.

Keith said: 'They've been caught . . . those swine have still got two horses.'

'Two horses won't be much use to them, *mon ami*,' D'Aran said.

Keith gestured towards the mules.

'Have they got to go?'

'*Oui* . . . I fear it must be so.'

In a sense the killing of the mules was more unpleasant than that of the horses. It was so easy. They were such extraordinarily philosophical creatures.

During the entire carnage they had remained quite still, there heads together like old men in conference. They even died with decorum. And Keith and D'Aran were able to make the end quick.

It had seemed longer, much longer, but they had been at the window less than two minutes when they turned from it to survey the room.

D'Aran breathed relief. '*Bon* . . . they are doing well.'

The legionnaires were indeed doing well. After D'Aran's sharp reprimand they had remembered and acted according to the carefully prepared plan.

Sergeant Vogel's body had been dragged under a wall. The guards were trussed with the ropes which had bound the legionnaires, and four heavy iron cots had been piled against the door. A fifth cot was in the process of being upended into position.

They formed a formidable barricade.

And as yet there had been no counter-action from Gallast and his remaining men. There had hardly been time.

One of the legionnaires had retrieved Vogel's pistol. D'Aran called him over.

'How many rounds have you?' he asked.

'Twenty-nine, *mon officier*. Two spare clips were in the sergeant's pocket and there are nine rounds in the magazine.'

D'Aran nodded. He examined his own gun. It was empty. Keith had one remaining cartridge in the breech. They crossed to the two guards — both still only semiconscious and badly bruised. They opened their ammunition pouches. Each contained two clips of ten.

D'Aran was looking thoughtful as he moved to the door to make a close inspection. With its reinforcement of iron, a battering ram would be needed to break it in. Satisfied, D'Aran gestured to the legionnaires. They gathered round him in the centre of the room. He spoke in a low pitched voice and slowly, so that all would clearly understand.

'I don't need to tell you how fortunate we've been, *mes soldats*. So far, audacity has succeeded, thanks particularly to two of you . . . '

He did not look at Keith, or towards the body of Vogel.

D'Aran continued: 'I have to tell you that we now hold the advantage. This room is a fort within a fort. The enemy now numbers only eight men — I am not including Professor Daak. There are twenty-seven of us. We have water. They have not. They have yet to find out that the body of one of their men is in the storage tank, plus a quantity of salt . . . '

There was a strained titter at this which D'Aran subdued with a frown.

He went on: 'The enemy has but one advantage — fire power. They possess our Lebels and practically limitless ammunition. We have only three Lugers and exactly seventy rounds. But it will be more than enough. For, *mes soldats*, we are no longer the prisoners. It is they who are captured . . .

'Think of their position. They cannot leave here because they have neither the

164

water nor the transport. Unless they want to be destroyed with us, they will have to allow us to send a message through to the High Command.

'So I do not think there will be more bloodshed. All we can do now is wait until I can speak to Gallast — and I think we shall be hearing from him very soon.'

3

So Softly Spoken . . .

Gallast had experienced a disturbed night. Professor Daak had been the cause. Daak was as unhappy in the nocturnal cool as he was in the daytime heat. He tossed restlessly on his bunk, which was placed under D'Aran's desk. Occasionally he dropped into an uneasy doze and then he rambled. He quoted problems in differential calculus in his high-pitched voice and provided the answers. He delivered disconnected extracts from a paper on nuclear physics. And when he awoke, he moaned about the condition of his heart and the agony in his head.

Gallast — only a few feet away on what had been D'Aran's bed — found it maddening. It made sleep almost impossible.

Several times he was on the point of shouting abuse at the paunchy Daak. But he refrained. For by now it was clear that the professor was seriously ill. And the professor represented the entire basis of the operation.

The secret penetration into Algeria on horseback, the daring and magnificent capture of a small Legion outpost, the carefully organised plane lifts . . . they would all be nothing if Daak could not complete his work.

At home men were eagerly awaiting the results of Daak's investigations into tomorrow's explosion.

Daak, with his phenomenal scientific brain, would be almost certain to deduce many secrets of the bomb after consulting his recording instruments. And the bodies of the legionnaires would give him further valuable data.

No, Daak must not be worried. Somehow he must be kept fit enough to work.

So Gallast tolerated the disturbances.

And it was not until towards dawn that the professor allowed him to fall into a light sleep.

He awoke to the sound of gunfire.

Gallast reacted instinctively.

He was pulling on his clothes before his brain began to work. Then, for a few confused seconds, he tried to assess the possibilities.

Had a Legion patrol arrived, through some hideous mischance? No — all the shooting was coming from within the building.

Had a legionnaire escaped? That was highly unlikely.

The whinnying of the horses gave him a vague clue. Then, through the window, he caught a glimpse of two animals careering round the compound. He heard the shouts of his men and the hoofbeats slowed and ceased.

He emerged into the compound in time to see the mules die. And to see the already dead horses.

Gallast did not allow himself the weakness of emotion. Nor did he continue theorising. He turned to one of his men who came running out of the building.

The man was obviously bewildered and frightened. He spluttered and waved a wild hand. Gallast struck his cheek with an open palm. It was a hard blow and the man staggered. But he lost his hysteria. He provided what information he had.

'The legionnaires . . . they've seized the bunk room!'

'Seized it! With six guards there!'

'Only three . . . Sarle went to look for the pitchers then two of us left to find him because the pitchers were behind the stove . . . '

Gallast extended a hand and gripped the man's jacket. He drew him towards him.

'Now,' he said, 'tell me exactly what you know since you released the legionnaires.'

The second description was more detailed.

'We were looking for Sarle when we heard the shooting. We had a glimpse of the inside of the room just before the door was locked. The Dutchman — the sergeant — was wounded, but he had a gun. The others had gone mad! They were rushing at our men . . . '

Gallast put a couple of quick questions.

The answers helped to complete an outline picture of what had occurred.

He stood completely still. Sweat dribbled down the sides of his powerful face. Fury and fear, the twin allies, struggled to gain possession of him.

He knew fury because of the seeming ineptitude of his men.

He knew fear because of what would almost certainly happen to him if he had to report failure of his critical operation. His own life, he knew, would have no more permanence than a naked flame in a storm.

For the second time that morning he conquered his emotions. But only after a mental battle which left him feeling weak, exhausted. Yet it also left his mind cold and clear.

What, he asked himself in the orthodox military manner, was the garrison's ultimate reason for shooting the horses and mules?

That was easy to answer. They intended to destroy all means of escape to the Keeba Foothills.

Had they succeeded?

Only partly. Two horses had survived. So — one of them could carry the nearly helpless Daak. The other could be laden with supplies. And he and his men would march . . .

He glanced at his watch. Nearly eight o'clock. Thirty-one hours before the explosion. Plenty of time, even on foot, to reach Keeba. And to prepare the complex protective trenches. The garrison could remain as they were. Bottled up in the bunk room, they could not interfere with the departure.

But . . .

Gallast was uneasy. Surely it could not be as simple as that? Why, for instance, had D'Aran not delayed the rising until tomorrow, when it would have been impossible to reach safety before the explosion?

D'Aran was young. It was obvious that he'd had little practical experience as an officer. But he was no fool. There must be a reason for choosing today of all days.

Gallast decided to talk with the Frenchman.

He was turning back into the building

when Daak emerged. Daak weaved rather than walked. His skin was yellow, save for blue patches under the round eyes. Gallast noticed that his clothes, which had formerly strained to contain his belly, now hung loose.

Daak said between heavy breaths: 'I've been talking to one of your men . . . he told me . . . '

Gallast subdued a sense of revulsion at the fat little man. At all costs Daak must be preserved.

'There's no need to worry, professor,' he said. 'It is a temporary inconvenience. No more. It merely means that we must leave here immediately. You will have a horse. The rest of us will walk.' Daak considered. He swallowed painfully and whined: 'But the legionnaires . . . we must overcome them first.'

Gallast misinterpreted the motive.

'It would not be worth the losses,' he said. 'Some of them are armed and they are in a strong position. No, professor, I'm afraid you must resign yourself to the fact that they won't stay in the fort to die. They may even try to follow us to the foothills. But in any case, there will be no human remains for you to examine after the explosion.'

Daak boggled for words. Then he erupted a spate of them.

'It's my instruments that I'm thinking about! What about my instruments? As soon as we leave here the legionnaires will come out of their room and smash them! I know they will . . . I know! And it will all have been for nothing . . . nothing . . . '

He was sobbing as he finished. But Gallast paid no attention. He was momentarily stunned.

Of course, Daak was right!

That must be one of the reasons why he had felt uneasy. That was one of the indefinite spectres which had haunted his mind. And it had been the preposterous Daak who had pointed it out to him! There was no time to waste.

Since the legionnaires certainly would not surrender, they must be destroyed. Every one of them must be killed before the fort was evacuated.

How?

Grenades were the answer. Splinter grenades which he had seen stored in the tiny magazine beneath D'Aran's room. One of them would destroy the bunk room door.

Two or three more tossed into the opening and nothing could survive in such a small space . . .

But before that happened he would spare a few minutes to talk with Lieutenant D'Aran. He was curious about one or two matters . . .

★ ★ ★

In the bunk room . . .

Keith said: 'Gallast's taking a hell of a time. Maybe he's not going to talk.'

D'Aran consulted his watch. Twelve minutes past eight. About fifteen minutes since the horses had been massacred.

'He'll be bringing up the grenades,' D'Aran said. 'He's bound to think of the grenades. But I'm sure he'll want to talk to me. Particularly when he realises that Sarle has vanished . . . '

174

The fort magazine was entered through a trapdoor in the floor of D'Aran's room. It was even smaller in area than the room itself, and less than four feet deep. In it was stored six spare Lebel rifles and bayonets, ten boxes of .300 ammunition, and one stout steel case containing two dozen de-fused hand grenades.

Gallast lifted out the case personally and unlocked it with the fort keys. The fuses were stored in a small compartment under the lid. He inserted them with skilful fingers, holding down each detonating spring as he did so. Then he pressed home the anchor pins, which made each grenade comparatively safe.

He had just finished the task when one of his men came in.

He said: 'Comrade Colonel — we cannot find Sarle!'

'Cannot find . . . are you sure he wasn't one of those left in the bunk room?'

'I'm certain, comrade colonel. He was guarding the legionnaires who went into the kitchen. Then he left to find the pitchers.'

'Then he must be in the fort! Are you all blind as well as being fools? No man can be lost for long in this place!'

'But he's not in the fort . . . '

'Of course he's in the fort! The main gates are barred. He could not have got out there without being seen. Or are you suggesting that he flew over the walls?'

The man shuffled and made no answer. Then Gallast asked: 'Did anyone see him leave the kitchen?'

'I — I don't know . . . '

'You don't know! Imbecile! All of you were handpicked for this operation. It was said that you were soldiers of outstanding daring and experience. Perhaps you are. But you also have the imaginations of donkeys! While I tried to get a little rest you allowed yourselves to be outwitted at every turn . . . '

He broke off, realising that his vituperation was costing valuable time. Then he indicated the grenades and added: 'Assemble those at the corner of the passage leading to the bunk room.

And tell every man to gather at the same place. Before I destroy the legionnaires I'm going to find out exactly what they've been doing . . . '

* * *

The voice of Colonel Gallast came through the door and the barricading beds. It was distinct, but it had a muffled quality. It said: 'Lieutenant D'Aran — are you there?'

A sigh spread among the legionnaires. Of relief. The vital hand was about to be played.

D'Aran gestured to the others to stay where they were. He walked nearer to the door and stopped a little to one side of it. Then, raising his voice slightly, he said: 'I thought I'd hear from you. You must have had an eventful morning, Gallast!'

'Yes, lieutenant, I won't deny that it has had its surprises.' He paused and added in a smoothly conciliatory fashion: 'Wouldn't it be best if you talked with me in your room?'

D'Aran was unaware of the fact, but his

answer caused Gallast to blink with surprise. He said: 'I'll probably be doing that very shortly, Gallast. But for the moment I'll stay where I am.'

'I see . . . as a soldier I want to say that you have surprised me. You have shown courage and audacity which is worthy of a better cause than the one you serve. But I am puzzled about some of the details of your tactics. Will you answer a few questions?'

'*Oui.*'

'Do you realise that with the two remaining horses we can still reach the foothills before the explosion? Why did you not wait until tomorrow, when our escape would have been impossible?'

D'Aran smiled. It was the first time he had smiled genuinely in weeks. He looked almost boyish again.

And he countered with another question. He asked: 'Have you had anything to drink this morning, Gallast?'

After an utter silence: 'I haven't — but will you explain?'

'You have no water. And you cannot travel far without water, can you, Gallast!'

'The . . . the tank . . . '

'One of your guards is at the bottom of the tank. I believe his name is Sarle. His body will have quite a contaminating effect, particularly in this climate. But, for good measure, *monsieur*, a large quantity of salt has been dropped in to keep him company!'

Another interval. Another absolute silence. It was broken by the sound of receding footsteps. Then quiet again. D'Aran found a carefully preserved cigarette stub. He lit it and waited . . .

Waited for nearly fifteen minutes.

The cigarette had been smoked down to the last centimetre and ground out when a voice which was a harsh parody of Gallast's normal tones said: 'We have managed to recover Sarle's body, lieutenant.'

'*Bon*. He would have to be removed some time and it is just as well that you have done the unpleasant work. Now are you convinced that you are trapped, Gallast?'

'Perhaps — perhaps I am convinced.'

'You appreciate that *we* have the only

pure water in the fort. It's in the pitchers that Sarle was said to have been seeking . . . now have you any other questions, Gallast?'

'No, I think not. I played for a great prize and the risks were great. I have lost. But in a sense you have lost also, lieutenant, for we will die together tomorrow afternoon.

D'Aran was smiling again as he said: 'That will not be necessary, Gallast. For our part, we intend to live. That is why we struck against you today, instead of waiting. We want plenty of time to contact the High Command, so that the explosion can be postponed.'

'And *how* do you intend to contact the High Command?'

'By the fort wireless, of course. How else?'

Softly, so softly that the legionnaires had to strain to hear, Gallast said: 'I destroyed the fort radio at two o'clock this morning . . .'

4

Collapse

Professor Daak heard it.

He had followed Gallast to the end of the corridor. He had propped himself against the wall. Mouth slack; pince-nez at an acute angle, he followed the exchanges.

And his breathing, always noisy, reached an agonising volume as the conversation progressed. He epitomised the distilled essence of terror as he listened to the references to the radio.

He stumbled to Gallast. Reaching up, he clawed at his shoulders with flabby, sweaty hands. And he gasped: 'Blundering cretin! I thought you were mad when you told me yesterday that you were going to destroy the wireless! But no one can tell Colonel Gallast anything! Oh no! Now see what you've done . . . we're trapped on top of a hydrogen bomb! We can't get away and we can't stop it exploding, so . . . '

Gallast half turned and regarded Daak with unconcealed contempt.

'We're not on top of it, as you put it. We're twenty-five miles off.'

'Twenty-five miles! It might as well be twenty-five inches! Do you know what will happen to us when that is detonated? Do you? I'll tell you! We'll dissolve! All that will be left of us will be a few pools of gristle and dried blubber. We . . . '

Gallast detached the clawing hands. Then he pushed Daak on the chest. It was not a violent push. But it was enough to knock the professor off balance.

Daak spun back against the wall. He stood there — staring at nothing. Then he fell on his face and was still.

Gallast bent down and felt under the moist shirt. There was a heartbeat — but a weak and irregular one. It did not matter. Daak was of no use now.

His men were gathered in a scared huddle a few yards away. They had moved up to hear what D'Aran said. They had heard more than enough.

Gallast jerked a thumb at them, then at Daak.

'One of you put the professor on his bunk,' he ordered.

No one moved.

'Did you hear what I said? Put the . . . '

A man whose clothing was dripping with water interrupted. This man had earlier had the unpleasant task of groping at the bottom of the tank while Gallast held his ankles.

He said: 'Put him there yourself, comrade colonel.'

Gallast regarded him steadily, with a form of detached interest. The rebel lowered his eyes. He was looking at the floor as he added sullenly: 'We're taking no more orders from you . . . no more orders from anyone.'

'And why won't you take orders from me?'

'Because you're an assassin. The professor has told us all we need to know. If it hadn't been for you, we could have sent a radio signal and got . . . '

The bullet from Gallast's Luger pierced the bridge of the man's nose and emerged at the top of his skull. He bore an expression of indignant astonishment as he died.

It was the unexpectedness of the killing rather than the killing itself which reduced the remaining six men to temporary impotence. But it was only temporary. After staring dumbly at Gallast, then at the body, they gave forth grunts of anger. Their hands strayed to their gun belts.

Gallast would not have survived another minute if D'Aran's voice had not come through the door.

D'Aran said: 'You'd better let me look at the wireless, Gallast.'

There was an easing of tension in the corridor.

After hesitating, Gallast pushed his gun in its holster and turned his back on his men.

'It's smashed, I tell you. I destroyed the valves. It can't be repaired.'

'There's a spare set of valves in the drawer of my desk. They are at the back. You probably have not noticed them.'

Gallast raised a hand to his forehead. It

shook. The others were shaking, too.

'Then it can be repaired!'

'Perhaps — if you have not destroyed any other components.'

'And we can contact your High Command . . . they'll have the explosion delayed! Thank you, lieutenant, thank you! I will make the repairs myself. You and your men will stay where you are. If you try to come out, you will be shot down.'

D'Aran's voice remained suave.

'No, Gallast, *I* will attend to the wireless. And *I* will send the signal. No help can reach us for at least twenty-four hours — and we have the water. Unless you want to die of thirst, you must do as I say.'

Gallast understood. He thought for a few moments. Then: 'I will make a bargain with you lieutenant — you allow us half of your water and we will leave the fort immediately. We will not attempt to harm you.'

D'Aran laughed.

'You're in no position to do any bargaining, Gallast. And that offer does not appeal to me at all. *Non* . . . you will resign yourself to the fact that I am again in command here. You are my prisoners. I am coming out of this room. But my men will remain inside. So long as you behave yourselves, my legionnaires will pass out to you at regular intervals just enough water to keep you alive. If there is any violence, the supply will stop. And if you attempt to attack us, the pitchers will be emptied on the floor. And if that happens, we may survive until help comes, for we have drunk our fill. But you are already thirsty, aren't you. It will be agony in a few hours. Do I make myself clear?'

Gallast's men had gathered round him, ignoring the swooning Professor Daak. They were again fingering their pistols. And the menace was directed at their leader.

One of them said: 'Let him repair the wireless . . . '

It started a chorus.

'We're beaten . . . '

'We need water . . . '

'I'd rather rot in a French prison than die of thirst . . . '

186

'Or be melted down by the bomb . . .'

Gallast felt a new surge of fury. This time it was entirely directed at his men — his handpicked shock troops. Men selected for their loyalty as well as their fighting abilities. In the moments of dire emergency they had broken. They were useless.

But he disguised his emotion.

'Come out, lieutenant,' he called. 'We'll do exactly as you say.'

★　★　★

D'Aran said to the legionnaires: 'Keep the water well away from the door. Pass them a cupful every two hours — no more.'

One of them asked: 'Shall we shut the door after you've gone?'

'*Non*, it won't be necessary. They won't dare to attempt any tricks while we hold the water. But none of them must be allowed in here. That understood?'

They nodded. But Keith was looking worried.

Keith said: 'I don't like the idea of you

going out there alone. Perhaps you'd better have company, *mon officier*.'

D'Aran put a hand on Keith's shoulder.

'I'll be quite safe, legionnaire. I will have a message transmitted within half an hour — if only the valves have been damaged. After that — we can only wait. And we may have to wait for quite a time, for the first task of the High Command will be to contact the scientists who are to detonate the bomb. They are some fifty miles south of Sanna in a remote area. It may be difficult.'

The legionnaires looked anxious. A Latvian said:

'What — what if they can't get the message through?'

D'Aran smiled reassurance.

'The High Command will manage that, *mon ami*. If they can't make radio contact, they'll send a plane. But that is the least of our worries. The main task at the moment is to get our own wireless working.'

Keith touched his hand. He said: 'Let me go with you, *mon officier*. You wouldn't understand. But . . . but I don't want to have to wait here while you're alone with those thugs. Gallast is clever. Anything could happen . . .'

'Nothing can happen. But come if you wish, legionnaire. Now — four men will take down the barricade!'

The iron beds were dragged away from the door. D'Aran and Keith unconsciously braced themselves when only the bolt stood between them and Gallast. D'Aran took a brief look round. Then he pulled back the bolt.

Gallast and his six men were waiting. Gallast came forward.

'There's no time to lose,' he said. 'I, too, understand wireless. I will help you.'

'You will stay here,' D'Aran told him. 'And so will your men.'

They were about to push past when Keith pointed to Professor Daak.

Daak was still on the floor. But he was now conscious. And he was making weak movements with his feet, as if trying to stand.

'I'll carry him to your room,' Keith said.

Without much difficulty he got the professor over his shoulder and followed D'Aran down the corridor.

They paused when about to enter the room. The place had assumed an even greater appearance of chaos. The extra bed had taken most of the remaining floor space. The magazine trapdoor was open. Papers — after being carefully read — had been thrust from the desk to the floor. And the radio table was a shambles of broken glass. Gallast had done a typically thorough job on the valves.

Keith lowered Daak on to his bed. The professor was recovering from his swoon. He sat upright and watched D'Aran open a desk drawer. When he saw the cartons of spare valves he blinked with hope and curiosity.

D'Aran carried the cartons to the radio table and there he made a quick but careful inspection. When he had finished he told Keith: 'I think we are fortunate.'

He set to work. He removed the broken valves from their sockets while Keith unpacked the replacements and placed them gently at his elbow.

Daak managed to get to his feet and watched intently. The atmosphere was heavy with expectancy.

At first none of them saw the score of brown men in tattered robes who easily climbed the low walls.

They did not see the Arabs gather on the ramparts and stare in bewilderment round the apparently empty fort.

No one saw them until a scream of panic came from one of Gallast's men. It was followed immediately by a shot from a Luger.

One of the Arabs — an aged man with a white beard — spun slowly on his heels before falling into the compound.

For a few seconds the tribesmen stared at him with a sheer lack of comprehension. Then one of them shouted. The call was taken up. A call of mad fury. Some waved their fists at the building. But most fumbled with their ancient muzzle-loading muskets.

Keith knew exactly what had happened. So did D'Aran. To those familiar with the command area, it was obvious.

This was an itinerant Bormone trading

party. One of the several groups of Arabs who roamed the area, buying merchandise from one village and selling to another. Sometimes, but not often, they called at Fort Ney and offered fresh oasis fruit in exchange for a few sous. They invariably commenced such commerce by displaying their wares to the sentries on the ramparts. But today they had found no sentries. And no sound of life, for the fort had been in complete silence as D'Aran worked on the radio. They must have concluded that Fort Ney was deserted. And, naturally enough, they had decided to investigate.

Had any of the garrison been the first to see them he would have realised this. But it must have been one of Gallast's men who had chanced to look outside.

And, in his ignorant panic, he had fired. He had killed.

Keith whispered: 'Oh, my God, the lunatics . . . ' Then, being nearest the door, he raced into the passage. So far no other shots had been fired from Gallast's party. But they were crouching near the outer door, gripping Lebels and Lugers.

Keith screamed: 'Don't shoot . . . they're harmless . . . they . . . '

But at that moment a volley of round shot came from the Arabs. The aim was wild. The slugs flattened against the outside wall.

But it was enough for Gallast. He turned a contorted face at Keith.

'Harmless, did you say. I don't believe you! I have a quick way of dealing with such riff-raff. Watch, legionnaire, and you will learn!'

Before Keith could appreciate his intentions, Gallast had stooped over the pile of grenades. As he straightened, he held one of them high in his right hand.

Keith did not attempt further argument. He almost threw himself at Gallast. He aimed a swinging left hand jab at his kidneys. If it had connected, Gallast would have dropped. But, as the punch travelled, a Luger butt came down on his wrist. Keith's entire arm became numb and momentarily useless.

He stood helpless as Gallast extracted the pin with his teeth.

He screeched, 'Don't . . . Don't . . . ' as

Gallast hurled the grenade through the outer door. Then, instinctively, he rushed back to D'Aran's room. The grenade had a five-second fuse. Five seconds to give warnings.

As he ran he shouted: 'Get under the window . . . '

But, as he crashed through the doorway he saw that D'Aran was already under cover. So was Daak. They had seen the grenade land in the centre of the compound.

Keith dropped flat as a harsh explosion, like the rattling of sheet iron, tore the air.

Almost immediately there was a cacophony of hideous sounds. The screams of the tribesmen. The echoing slash of hot shrapnel against the walls. And, worst of all, a shattering of wood and glass which told of the end of the radio.

5

Isolation

The explosive effect of a hand grenade is lateral. The jagged splinters of metal fly outwards, but only slightly upwards. For that reason the Arabs suffered remarkably few casualties. Standing as they were on the ramparts, most of the fragments spent their energy against the wall below them.

One of their number had a foot almost sliced off. Two others were less seriously wounded about the legs. The rest escaped.

Keith saw this as he peered out of the window. Then he turned to speak to D'Aran. But D'Aran was moving out of the room. His gun was in his hand. Keith followed.

Gallast was standing by the outer door, tossing a fresh grenade from hand to hand. As he watched the huddled, temporarily paralysed Arabs, his big face reflected a peculiarly brutalised satisfaction. Beneath his ostensible polish, Gallast was a typical thug. This was the type of situation which appealed to him. The murder of semi-defenceless people, supported by only the thinnest veneer of justification, naturally enabled him to forget all other matters.

He looked with some surprise at D'Aran's gun. Then he said: 'We won't have any more trouble with that offal, lieutenant. But I think perhaps another grenade.'

Gallast broke off as he felt a point of pressure in the centre of his stomach. It was the muzzle of D'Aran's gun.

And D'Aran said: 'Put the grenade down!'

'Lieutenant, I . . . '

'Put it down!'

Gallast obeyed. There was a quality in D'Aran's voice which left no choice.

Meantime, Keith stood against the wall. He, too, was holding a Luger. He glanced at Gallast's men. But there did not seem to be much danger of interference from them. They were moving away into the shadows.

D'Aran said in a dangerous, silky way: 'Do you realise that the offal, as you describe them, are French subjects?'

There was no pretence about Gallast's astonishment.

'They are barbarians!'

'They are subjects of the French Empire. As such, they receive the same rights and protection as any person born in metropolitan France. By occupation, they are peaceful traders.'

'Don't be ridiculous, lieutenant! They were rushing the walls.'

'Fool! They were coming in to find why this post was apparently unoccupied. Look at them, Gallast! Do they seem like warriors? Are they equipped as warriors?'

Gallast licked his lips several times. His eyes narrowed.

'You're sure they are traders?'

'*Oui*.'

'Then no great harm has been done. It seems that only one of them has been seriously hurt.'

D'Aran paused before saying with slow precision: 'The radio cannot be repaired,

Gallast. Not now. A fragment from your grenade has ruined it finally!'

From his superior height, Gallast looked down on D'Aran. The sudden tightening of the skin over his broad cheekbones was the only indication of emotion.

Then he said: '*I shouldn't worry too much about that, lieutenant.*'

'Shouldn't worry . . . '

D'Aran, being French, could not always conceal his feelings. He did not conceal them now. He took an involuntary backward step.

And he had a sudden weird feeling. A feeling of unforeseen insecurity. As if the earth had disintegrated beneath him. And he knew — knew from the essence of his soul — that for the past minute Gallast had been playing with him. *Oui*, playing! Talking to gain time. But why? Why?

As his confused brain groped for an answer, he realised that Gallast was no longer staring at him, Gallast was looking towards the ramparts.

D'Aran followed his gaze. At first he saw nothing only the huddled Arabs. And he wondered why they had not yet fled over the wall to safety. They ought to have recovered from their paralysing fright by now.

But they were still. There was not a flicker of a limb among them.

Then D'Aran saw the reason.

Four Lebels were being aimed at them. Lebels held by Gallast's men. Two were on each side of the Arabs, some ten yards distant from them and on the ramparts, too.

The tribesmen, pressed together and armed only with their unwieldy muskets, could make no resistance without immediately being shot down.

D'Aran felt an ache in his heart as he realised what had happened. While he had been talking to Gallast the four men — acting under orders — had moved out of the rear of the building. There they had mounted the ramparts, then converged on the Arabs without being seen until the last moment.

But the original question remained — why?

Why hold these harmless Bormones in the fort?

Gallast supplied the answer. He did it with smooth satisfaction.

'You constantly underestimate me, lieutenant,' he said. 'The moment I first saw the Arabs I appreciated a vital fact. Can you guess what it is? No! Then I'm afraid your conscience is clouding your judgement. I realised that they must have arrived on horseback. And they must have supplies of water . . . '

He broke off to study D'Aran's tense face. D'Aran said quietly: 'Go on, Gallast.'

'There is not much more to say, is there? I intend to take their horses and water — then move on to the safety of the foothills, as planned. You, of course, will be left here — as corpses. Since we still cannot risk any damage to the instruments.'

A voice spoke to D'Aran. A nebulous, disembodied voice which seemed to come out of infinity. It said: '*Lieutenant D'Aran, perhaps you can be forgiven for being a thief. But not for being a fool. You seized the advantage. Then you threw it away because you let your enemy*

200

think faster than you. Do you not remember what you were taught at St. Maixent? You were taught that tactics are the art of adapting unexpected circumstances to one's own advantage . . . '

He shook his head. The voice faded. But he was left with a sense of infantile helplessness. Without realising it, he let his gun fall slightly as he asked: 'Why did you shoot at them, Gallast? And why the grenade?'

'The shot was pure excitement on the part of one of my men. But the grenade was a calculated act on my part. Having at once assessed the possibilities, I saw that it might be fatal if I permitted the Arabs to gain entry to the fort. After all, I have only six men. I had to do something which would halt the Arabs and terrify them for a few seconds until we could get them covered. And, of course, I was careful to give you the impression that I was merely acting in ignorance and panic.'

D'Aran was gaining control of himself. He said: 'Aren't you being optimistic? You have four men on the ramparts. That means that besides yourself you have only two others. We number nearly thirty. We can easily deal with you, Gallast.'

He did not answer verbally. Instead he looked inside the building and smiled. It was an insulting, patronising smile.

D'Aran looked, too. And he understood the completeness of the rout.

One of Gallast's men was standing at the angle of the wall. A grenade was balanced in his hand. It would be simple — too simple — for him to snatch out the pin and lob that grenade into the bunk room where the legionnaires were waiting.

The other man had appeared directly behind Keith. He was gripping a Lebel. It was aimed at the centre of Keith's back.

Even as D'Aran watched, Keith dropped his Luger and raised his hands. He did so after receiving a snarled order, and after glancing over his shoulder to establish his utter impotence.

Keith met D'Aran's eye. Each understood the other's feelings. This was the nadir of misery, of futility, of humiliation. All the careful planning, the patience, the controlling of tortured nerves, was for nothing. Why? Basically, because a party of Arab traders had chanced to arrive with horses and water. Arrived at a time when a shortage of horses and water was the master weapon which the garrison was deploying.

It was when D'Aran's eyes and mind were thus distracted that Gallast disarmed him. He did so with the confident speed of a man well versed in such matters.

He was still idly tossing a grenade from hand to hand. Suddenly the steel oval was flicked upwards, striking D'Aran on the mouth. For an instant, D'Aran thought that all of them were going to be killed there and then.

Then he realised that the grenade pin was still locked in place. It was safe.

But, as he staggered back, Gallast grabbed the Luger barrel and twisted it inwards.

D'Aran felt an excruciating pain as he tried to hold on. He could not do so. When he released his grip Gallast hit him on the jaw.

As he sprawled on the ground Gallast laughed at him. The Luger was aimed at him.

And Gallast was saying: 'I'm going to shoot you, lieutenant. I'm going to shoot you now. And the man with you. Then we are going to throw grenades into the bunk room.'

6

The Weary Heart

Keith heard the sentence of death. But he also heard something else.

The sound of heavy breathing. Of uncertain footsteps. Professor Daak was stumbling along the corridor towards them.

Then Daak was with them.

He turned the corner, rested a shoulder against the wall. His pince-nez was no longer on his nose and he blinked short-sightedly.

Keith edged round so that the Lebel rifle was aimed at his ribs rather than his back. The guard did not appear to notice the movement. He was half occupied in taking darting glances at Daak. So was Gallast. And D'Aran.

For Daak was quivering on the edge of hysteria.

His pink face was convulsed like the

heaving of a turgid sea. Tears were forming in his round eyes. He began to whimper. And to utter disconnected, meaningless words.

The grenade explosion had been the last straw so far as the professor was concerned.

Gallast made an effort to control his annoyance. He said to him: 'Go back to your bunk. Rest for a while. You have nothing to worry about. We have horses now and water.'

But Daak did not appear to hear. He rubbed moist, dim eyes with the back of his hand. He fought to control himself — and with some effect, for his words suddenly began to make sense.

'I can't go on,' he slobbered. 'I can't! I'm sick and weary. My heart . . . it is weary, too . . . ' He broke off, then said to Gallast: 'You have horses and water? How is that?'

'They are outside the walls,' Gallast said. 'They belong to our Arab visitors. Now do as I advise and get . . . '

Daak interrupted wildly. His high-pitched voice rose to a piercing falsetto.

'Then let us get away from here! If we start now we may get out of the danger zone in time . . . we must do it . . . we must . . . I can't stay in this place any longer!'

'Professor Daak,' Gallast said with greater emphasis, 'return to your bunk immediately. I will speak to you later.'

Despite his condition, Daak recognised the insult in the words. And he reacted to it.

Bunching his fleshy little fists he shrieked: 'Don't dare talk to me so! I will not be addressed in such a manner by a — a piffling colonel. You forget that this is an operation for a scientific purpose. I cannot achieve that purpose. I'm too ill. We must return immediately by the same way that you came. On horseback! I insist!'

It was a critical moment for Gallast.

In military parlance, he had achieved an unconsolidated manoeuvre. Horses and water were to hand, but not yet under direct control. The Arabs were cowering on the ramparts, but a mere four rifles kept them so. The legionnaires were obeying orders by staying in their bunk room, but they had not yet been eliminated. The lieutenant and the English legionnaire were at his elbow and ripe for killing, but they were still very much alive.

And now, into the cockpit of the crisis, a semi-hysterical and utterly demoralised Daak had blundered.

It was obvious that if Daak were to witness any further violence he would lose his reason. And that would be a tragedy for the state both now and in the future. His knowledge, his ability, were priceless. So Gallast saw very clearly that he could not kill D'Aran and Keith while the quivering professor watched. But firm measures would have to be used to induce him to get back to the room.

Gallast was still watching D'Aran as he said to Daak: 'We cannot return by the way we came, professor. In your condition you would not survive the journey. It would take us two weeks to reach our agents on the coast. No — we will take the much shorter trip to the safety of the foothills. There you can rest for a few days. And, when it is safe to do so, we will return here and you will compile the data from your instruments. After that . . . the plane will come for us and we will reach Europe in comfort, with our mission completed.'

It was an unfruitful attempt at firm conciliation. The professor threshed his fists.

'It's no use, I tell you! I won't stay here! I can't stand it! The heat's killing me, and the tension . . . the violence . . . they are driving me insane! I order you to return now, on my own responsibility.'

Gallast said in a voice of grating calmness: 'And suppose you achieved the journey, professor — what explanation would you give? How would you explain that you had not even waited for the nuclear explosion?'

'I'd — I'd tell them the truth. That I feel ill . . . '

'And I would tell them that you were an errant coward and that you betrayed the state because of that cowardice. I would deny that you were ill while out here.'

'You wouldn't do that! It's not true! I *am* ill!'

'None the less, that is what I would say, professor. And, valuable though you are to the state, I think they would be quite drastic with you. You would certainly be shot.'

Of a sudden, Daak's normally heavy breathing became softer, less audible.

But his entire body quivered, as if actuated by a spring. There was a quintessence of hate in his oval face.

Then he hurled himself at Gallast.

No other word would accurately describe the action. Literally, he projected himself from the ground before crashing against Gallast's chest, his soft fingers clawing for the throat.

In his maddened condition, Daak had achieved a physical feat which would have been quite impossible under normal circumstances. It was not the sort of reaction that any of them could reasonably have expected.

For that reason, Gallast was taken completely by surprise.

He staggered back. He put up his left

hand in an effort to thrust Daak off while at the same time trying to keep his gun levelled at D'Aran. It was a natural impossibility.

D'Aran swerved out of range of the pistol. He lashed out with his boot. It contacted Gallast's hip bone. He gave out a grunt of pain as he sank to his knees. The grunt became a loud cry as D'Aran stamped on his gun hand. He rolled on his back after letting the gun go free. He was lying in that position when D'Aran kicked again — this time at his close-cropped head. The head twitched. Then he was still.

Keith moved simultaneously but independently of D'Aran.

During his rush through the air Daak passed between Keith and the man with the Lebel. There was perhaps an entire second in which Keith did nothing. A second used to absorb the situation.

Then he saw that the Lebel was no longer aimed directly at him. It was quivering uncertainly in the direction of Daak.

Keith grabbed the barrel at a point just

in front of the back sight. At the same time he twisted and wrenched. The rifle bucked violently as the pressure on the guard's finger discharged a bullet, which flattened itself between the join of the wall and the floor. But the violent movement caused by that bullet served a purpose. It was the final thrust needed to get the rifle away from the man's hands.

Keith was then holding the Lebel so that the heavy butt was directly under the guard's chin.

He brought the butt up in a whistling arc. It proceeded on its course after the jawbone had been broken and two of the cervical vertebrae dislocated.

The man who had been standing beside the grenades rushed at Keith, pulling a Luger from his belt as he did so.

It was a bad mistake. If he had held his ground while drawing the gun, Keith's activities would have come to an abrupt conclusion. But as it was, Keith closed with him while the weapon was still only half out of the deep military holster. And, since the guard was pulling at it, he had only one hand available for immediate defence.

It was not enough.

He was a perfect target.

Keith used the edge of his open hand. It sliced against the front of his neck, directly on the larynx. It was a cruel, killing form of unarmed attack. But this was no occasion for niceties. The man's face became a pale shade of blue before he dropped across his pile of grenades.

Keith felt a sudden sense of exhilaration. Of returning confidence. Of release from the bondage of fear.

A thought flashed through his mind.

'I'm not yellow,' he thought, as he turned to go to the aid of D'Aran. 'I can't be yellow because I'm not afraid now . . .'

He saw that D'Aran was not in need of help. D'Aran was already leaving the inert Gallast and moving into the passage.

Keith knew what the lieutenant was about to do. He did it for him. He ran panting towards the bunk room.

The legionnaires were pressed near the door. Their faces were baffled and anxious. But they were obeying D'Aran's order to remain there.

'Get to hell out of it,' Keith bawled in rich English vernacular.

Few of them understood his words. But the meaning was made clear by wild gestures. The garrison stormed out of the bunk room, still unsure of exactly what had happened, or of what was expected of them.

D'Aran halted them as the foremost reached the corridor leading to the outer door.

He pointed to the three guns — two on the ground, one half out of a holster. And to the fallen Lebel. The sign was enough. Four legionnaires armed themselves.

'Stay where you are,' D'Aran ordered.

He returned to the door and looked towards the ramparts. Keith, who had affected not to hear the command, was at his side.

The Arabs were no longer still, although they remained on the ledge. They were gesticulating, chattering, showing every aspect of scared indecision. Some, more courageous than the others, were making menacing movements with their muskets towards the four guards.

And the guards on each side had dropped to their knees, so as to sight more precisely at the mob.

D'Aran muttered: '*Dieu* . . . there'll be a massacre!'

It certainly seemed so. If the four guards opened fire at the tribesmen from that range, the result would be utter carnage. And — because they were obviously very frightened themselves — they intended to do just that. Their attention must be distracted immediately.

D'Aran and Keith fired together at the four men.

But the range was too long for accurate pistol fire. The slugs travelled wide and low. Yet the brief volley served its purpose.

The guards looked away from the Arabs and towards the two men at the compound door.

Then the Arabs charged.

They divided off into two sections like a disintegration of quicksilver. They were upon the four guards before they had time to turn back their heads.

The guards disappeared into twin seas of swirling, tattered robes. They remained invisible for nearly a minute, while the Arabs did their work in silence.

And when the Arabs drew back, Keith felt sick. He looked away. So did D'Aran.

D'Aran forgot his revulsion as he gazed again at the Arabs.

He said: '*Sucre!* Stop them!'

Then he shouted uselessly.

The tribesmen were clambering over the wall and dropping outside the fort. Presently, the only token of their visit were the four still bodies and the old Bormone who had died earlier.

D'Aran ran towards the gate, shouting to them. He used desperate persuasions in an effort to bring them back.

But his voice was drowned by the thudding of their horses' hooves. When D'Aran could be heard again, the hoofbeats had faded into the empty distance.

He returned slowly to the building. He ignored the unconscious body of Gallast. He gave scant attention to Professor

Daak, who was crouching in a semi-swoon.

As he entered the doorway, he said to the legionnaires: '*Mes amis*, I hoped that those Arabs, at least, might have been saved. I wanted to warn them that they must leave this area immediately. But since they would not listen, I fear they will die. As for us — we must start our march to the foothills.'

He examined his watch. He was astonished to see the hands indicating two o'clock. The hour was confirmed by the position of the sun.

D'Aran continued: 'We have only twenty-five hours to get there and prepare protective positions, but I think it can be done. And let us thank God for one great mercy — we have enough water for the march . . .'

Professor Daak interrupted. He had been listening dazedly to D'Aran's words. Still crouching and looking like an obese and thrashed animal, he whimpered: 'What about me? I can't march!'

D'Aran regarded him with open contempt.

217

'We still have two horses. You can use one of them.'

There was an uneasy movement among the legionnaires. They were looking at each other in a strained, transfixed manner. But D'Aran did not notice, for Keith was speaking to him.

Keith made a gesture towards Gallast and the other surviving guards.

'What about them, *mon officier?*'

Like most Frenchmen, D'Aran was essentially practical. He seldom wasted sympathy on undeserving causes.

'We will leave them here. I would like to leave the professor, too, but he is more valuable than the others.'

By now there was a blatant atmosphere of tension in the corridor where the legionnaires were gathered. And they were no longer looking at each other. They were staring at the ground.

D'Aran asked quietly: 'What's the matter, *mes braves?*'

There was no answer. Yet it was obvious that they had something to say.

'*Tiens!* Have you swallowed your tongues?'

Another silence.

Then one of the legionnaires raised his hand. He stared past D'Aran as he said: 'We cannot march to the foothills, *mon officier*. We will have to stay here, too. We have only a few pints of water.'

'Only a few pints! You had two pitchers!'

'I know, *mon officier*. But some splinters from the grenade came into the bunk room. They smashed one pitcher into pieces. The other was damaged, but we managed to save a little water in it . . .'

7

The Dark Hours

D'Aran strode quickly into the bunk room. The garrison followed. He stood in the centre of the floor and looked carefully around.

He saw the clean scars in the stonework where the steel fragments had ricocheted off the inside top of the window.

He saw the vicious furrows where they had skidded across the floor.

He saw a scattering of broken pottery, which was all that remained of one pitcher.

He saw the other with an open crack from the lip to the middle. It contained about four pints.

At his feet he saw a large and slightly steaming patch of moisture — of wasted liquid.

He turned to the legionnaires, lips twisted in a parody of a smile.

'Was anyone hurt?'

And as he asked the question he knew it to be ridiculous. It did not matter if the fragments had wounded anyone. Nothing mattered, but it was tradition which prompted the enquiry. The tradition, hammered home at St. Maxient, that an officer's first concern must be for his men.

'No one was wounded, *mon officier*. It was a miracle. Only the water was lost.'

Only the water!

He wanted to laugh. Laugh loud and wildly, releasing into the hot still air the suppressed frenzy within him. But he could not do so. He must not do so. Soon, as the hours ticked away towards the inevitable doom, panic would tempt the men. Madness would goad them. Only he, Andre D'Aran, the cheap thief, could preserve some semblance of discipline. Why? Because of the uniform he wore. A grimy uniform on an undeserving body! But it still symbolised the glorious traditions of the officers of France. *Non*, he must not break. He, D'Aran the thief, must be calm and strong . . .

He spoke to the men — in a voice which was little above a whisper. But it contained no hint of weakness.

'*Mes braves*, I wish I could offer you hope, but I cannot. The water that remains would scarcely be enough for two of us on such a march. But we have a consolation, have we not? We have defeated the enemies who came within our walls. They sought to learn secrets which such men should never know. They have failed and in that respect we have kept faith. Our main regret must be that we have been unable to warn the Arabs in our command area of the explosion. Many of them will die at three o'clock tomorrow. As for us . . . we will die, too. Let us do so like men . . . '

Despite his youth, despite those conflicting lines of care on his face, there was a calm dignity about Andre D'Aran, the thief, as he walked slowly out of the bunk room.

★ ★ ★

Nine o'clock . . .

The moon was up, touching Fort Ney with lights of gold. A traveller, chancing on the place at that time, might have said: 'Here is a tiny haven set in a sea of sand. It is a place of peace . . . '

But there was no peace within Fort Ney that night. The cauldron of hell was brewing. And it was being stirred by Legionnaire Rhuttal, the Latvian.

Rhuttal was an orator, just as the late Sergeant Vogel had been a reader. Rhuttal would speak with fluency and at great length on any conceivable subject.

He was never in any way deterred by the fact that his opinions were usually arrant nonsense and his authorities merely the products of his own vivid imagination.

Rhuttal loved words and ideas, so long as they were his own. And his comrades tolerated him with good humour. For in the normal way Rhuttal was harmless. In the normal way Rhuttal was merely one of the world's great army of windbags.

But, given a suitable opportunity, such

men can be intensely dangerous. Legionnaire Rhuttal had found such an opportunity.

He was surrounded by strained and frightened men. Men who were waiting . . . waiting to die. Men who felt the acid of fear burning at their vitals. Such men will listen gladly to anyone who speaks with assurance and offers hope.

Rhuttal was doing that.

He stood at the top end of the room, the moon shafts on his back, his face illuminated by the flickering oil lamps. The legionnaires sprawling on the cots were listening intently.

'How do we know that there's no water in the foothills?' Rhuttal was asking. 'We don't know. There may be water there. So why must we stay in this place, waiting to be frizzled alive? Why, I ask you? Let us leave for the foothills now!'

Keith rose from his bunk. He said: 'You talk like a fool. We'd never reach the foothills without water to drink on the way. It's better to wait here . . . '

Rhuttal turned fanatical eyes on Keith. 'Very well, you may be right . . . '

'I know I'm right, and so do you.'

'Then, I say, let one of us take half the remaining water and set out for the Keeba foothills alone. It is better that one of us has a chance of life than that all of us should die!'

There was a tentative rumble of agreement.

Keith was still standing as he said icily: 'And who would be the lucky man? Are you thinking of yourself, Rhuttal?'

Rhuttal flushed and glared. Then he said with less force: 'I am ready to take the risk. Surely none of you would stand in my way, since it is my plan?'

There was a wave of stark, humourless laughter. Then a babble of eager talk.

A black American, who had gambling in his blood said: 'Ah figure we could draw for it.'

General agreement.

Keith turned on them, temper rising.

'Our orders are to stay here! We all heard what D'Aran said.'

'To hell with D'Aran,' Rhuttal said, eager now to grasp at this slender chance. 'We'll have a draw. There are two pints of water left. The man who wins will leave with half of it and a horse.'

'The horse won't last long. Both of them are frantic with thirst now.'

The American came in again. He was a man with ideas, too.

'Ah guess the horses could use the water from the tank. That water sure would poison us right away, but them nags wouldn't know no harm for a long time.'

Keith was forced to admit to himself that this was true. No one had thought of letting the animals have the contaminated tank water.

There was an excited chorus from the legionnaires.

' . . . How far are the foothills?'

' . . . Thirty miles.'

' . . . The horses could carry two men each!'

' . . . And be there in a few hours!'

' . . . Before there was time to be thirsty.'

Keith stood on the end of his cot. He bawled for silence as the tumult died away.

'You're forgetting two things besides the lieutenant's orders,' he said. 'First, those foothills are only slopes of sand. There may be no water there for the men who arrive. Second, you've got to dig special protective ditches against the nuclear explosion. If you don't, you die just the same. Four weak and thirsty men wouldn't have the strength for that kind of work!'

For a few seconds they considered in silence.

Rhuttal broke it. He shouted: 'Let's take a chance. Anything's better than all staying in this trap!'

Another rumble of agreement.

One legionnaire produced a dirty writing pad. He tore the paper into small identical squares, ready for the draw. On four of the squares he scrawled a cross. He was folding them as he said to Keith: 'Are you in with us?'

Keith shook his head.

'I'm not running out. Every man who joins that draw is yellow! Yes, yellow! I think D'Aran would be glad to be rid of them!'

There was a sudden, ugly silence.

But Keith was not aware of it. He knew only that he, Keith Tragarth, the man who ran away, was calling a garrison of legionnaires yellow! Fantastic! Yet, truly, he was not afraid. And *they* were . . .

The black American shambled up to Keith. He was a big man, with the face and shoulders of a pugilist.

He said: 'Ah don't let no one call me yellow, bud. Mebbe you'd like to take them words right back.'

Keith stepped down from the cot, his fists bunching. The last thing he wanted at the moment was a brawl, but he wasn't going to run away from one . . .

There it was again!

He wasn't going to run away!

Yes, he, Keith Tragarth, was a changed man! He *was* a man!

A couple of legionnaires stepped between them. One of them said: 'We ought to settle this another way. We can settle it in front of D'Aran . . . tell him to his face just what we're doing. Perhaps he'll agree with us.'

Keith nodded.

'We'll see D'Aran,' he said.

His fountain pen was smashed.

D'Aran had found it crushed on the floor of his room. Perhaps either he or Gallast had stood on it during that first fight a week ago. But it was a pity. It had been a good pen. His family had saved to buy it for him when he won his scholarship to St. Maixent . . .

Now he would have to write his report on that typewriter. The machine with four missing keys.

D'Aran lifted it from the floor, put it on his desk. He regarded it without confidence.

Fortunately, three of the absent keys were numerals. They need not be used. The other was the letter 'G', which would result in tiresome delays over the name 'Gallast'. The initial letter would have to be written in pencil afterwards. He must remember to leave space for it.

Before sitting down, D'Aran told himself: 'You're a fool to bother about writing a report. However well you protect it, it will probably be destroyed in the explosion. No one will ever read it.'

Then he muttered an answering argument: 'But it *may* survive. I could roll it tightly and push it into the breech of a Lebel . . . In any case, it's my duty to leave a report. If I don't, there's no possibility of the High Command ever knowing what has happened. And I owe it to my men. They will die tomorrow; some are dead already, but their names deserve to live in the story of France . . . And the world ought to know why the Arab populations were not warned . . . '

He inserted a sheet of thick, rough paper in the ancient machine. He tapped slowly, wearily. Heavily, too, for the ribbon was almost as old as the typewriter.

There were slight disturbances, but they did not distract him.

Daak was again on his bunk, each intake of his breath producing a penetrating rasp. His hands were folded symbolically over his heart. He stared vaguely at the ceiling, where a few sandflies were buzzing round the lamp. He was too afraid to express his fear.

Gallast was on the floor, near the radio

table, legs and arms bound. But for the moment there was little need for such precautions. He was still unconscious after the kick on his skull. He had been thus for more than seven hours. Perhaps he would never wake up. In which case he would be lucky. Only one other member of his party lived. He was similarly bound and in the corridor.

D'Aran worked on. The first sheet was headed *Zone Zero: Fort Ney Operational Report*.

The words did not come easily to him. It was an effort to concentrate. He wanted to think about other things.

About those fifty thousand francs . . .

What had happened when the safe was opened?

Had he been condemned immediately? Or had they — poor fools — decided to await his return before reaching a decision?

And Lucinne.

What was she doing now? It was nearly nine-thirty. Perhaps, at this very moment, she would be in that restaurant on the edge of Tala Baku. With some other officer. Perhaps with that colonel. *Bien!* He was welcome to her. *Slut!*

He was glad to hear the clatter of boots in the corridor. Then the firm knock on the door. So the garrison wanted to speak with him. He had expected it. No doubt some of them wanted to quit their post. That would be worse than useless. It would look bad, cowardly. He would try to stop it, if he could . . .

'*Entre!*'

Four legionnaires came in. One was Tragarth. The others included the black American and Rhuttal, the Latvian. The fourth man was a German.

D'Aran suddenly recalled a clause in the French Army Manual of Discipline. It stated very clearly that legionnaires had a right to speak to an officer at any reasonable time. But not in groups. Only individually. This was a clear contravention of that clause. But it did not matter.

Nothing mattered — except finishing that damned report and keeping one's nerve.

The four men stood to attention. That was good. It showed that some fragments of discipline still remained. The others clustered outside the open door.

'*Repos!*' D'Aran said quietly. They stood at ease. Keith spoke.

'*Mon officier,* some of the — '

But Rhuttal interrupted. Rhuttal would not miss such an opportunity for making an oration.

To give due credit, he outlined the situation fairly, laying particular stress on the possibility of using the two horses. But, because D'Aran was a far more intelligent man than Rhuttal, he had comprehended all the points long before the exposition was concluded. That gave him time to think, while the Latvian's voice rose and fell.

But there was one man in that room who never ceased to listen.

It was Daak.

The weak, the ailing Professor Daak, who desperately wanted to live. It was he who spoke immediately after the Latvian.

He said: 'What the man says about the horses is true. They are not so susceptible to stomach toxins as men. And the salt in the water will not do them any immediate harm: — though later it will drive them mad.'

They regarded him with surprise.

D'Aran said: 'Thank you for your assurance, professor, but I can deal with these matters myself. Whether any men leave this fort or not, one thing is certain — you will stay here.'

Daak blinked weakly. He groped for his pince-nez, found it on the blanket. When it was in position, he said: '*I* am an old man . . . I did not come here willingly . . . you are soldiers, so you expect to die. Surely you will give me the chance to live? Listen . . . I'll make a bargain! If I am allowed to leave with three legionnaires for the foothills, I will willingly surrender to the French after the explosion. And I will reveal everything — I promise it. I know a great deal about thermonuclear explosions. I could — '

Keith was watching him. Staring at Daak in a fixed, unseeing way.

Nine words which the professor had used were hammering in his brain.

'*I know a great deal about thermonuclear explosions . . .*'

That was what he had said.

There was nothing new in that. Obviously, he must have a vast knowledge of the subject. Then why were those words repeating themselves? Crashing in his head, as if trying to tell him something which was not contained in the simple context!

Why?

In the moment of realisation, Keith thought he was going to collapse. The implications were almost beyond toleration.

He moved towards D'Aran, his face taut and twisted. '*Mon officier* . . . just for one minute, can I speak to you alone?'

D'Aran hesitated. Then he nodded as he rose from behind the desk.

'If you insist, legionnaire,' he said. 'We'll go into the compound.'

★ ★ ★

They were absent for fully fifteen minutes. And when they returned Keith's face was flushed. D'Aran's features betrayed a mingling of hope and doubt.

The legionnaires in the room and the corridor crowded closer.

Daak was blinking on the side of his cot. It was Daak to whom D'Aran spoke.

He said gently: 'Are you sure that your knowledge would be of value to us, professor?'

Daak's face suffused with hope.

'Most certainly! I think I have been following a different basis of calculation, but that would make my conclusions more valuable to the West.'

'And you are prepared to betray your own country?'

'I — I have changed my views. In my soul, I have always sympathised with the West. It would not be a betrayal.'

D'Aran nodded cynically.

Then he said slowly and precisely: '*Could you defuse a thermo-nuclear bomb?*'

Only the flies were unaffected. They continued to buzz round the oil lamp.

It seemed that all the men there ceased to live. For transitory seconds they did not breathe, they did not move. Then, like animals stirring after hibernation, they gave out a long, deep sigh.

Except Daak.

He remained immobile, his jaw slack.

D'Aran moved closer to him.

'Answer me, professor! Could you defuse a thermonuclear bomb? *Could you?*'

Daak closed his jaw, only to open it again as he croaked: 'I — I don't know, lieutenant! I don't think so . . . '

'But you boasted of your knowledge just now.'

'It was a true boast!'

'Then if we were to get you to the Sanna proving ground, surely you could render the explosive harmless!'

Daak raised both hands in a flabby gesture.

'No! You don't understand such things! It would be necessary to immobilise the atom triggering. To do that I would have to know the type of neutron and nucleus employed. Without such knowledge I would be working in the dark. I might even set the bomb off prematurely.'

His words sounded impressively final.

D'Aran said: 'The bomb will be

exploded through electrical contact, will it not?'

'Yes — almost certainly. Electricity is not quite the element used, but it is near enough.'

'It will be carried on a cable?'

'Certainly. There can be no other way.'

'Could we break the cable?'

Daak jerked to his feet.

'God, no! The cable will certainly be armoured! But in any case, an attempt to sever it would be more dangerous than meddling with the bomb itself!'

'Then it seems that you must meddle with the bomb, professor!'

He whimpered.

'I can't . . . I wouldn't have one chance in a hundred . . . '

'You'll have no chance at all if you do not,' D'Aran said. 'It is now ten o'clock. We have seventeen hours to reach the Sanna Oasis and defuse the bomb. If the horses hold out, we will get there before dawn. That ought to allow you plenty of time. But you can be assured of one thing, professor — if you fail, I won't blame you!'

There was a trickle of nervous laughter.

Then a legionnaire said: 'Who's going with you, *mon officier?*

'Legionnaire Tragarth.'

The legionnaires said suspiciously: 'Suppose Daak succeeds — what then? You'll die of thirst. So will we.'

D'Aran shook his head.

'I don't think so. If there is no explosion at three o'clock, we can be sure that many people will rush to Sanna at great speed to find what's amiss. I will be waiting for them . . . I will tell them. Relief will soon reach you.'

He seemed satisfied.

D'Aran turned again to Daak: 'We will carry water for you alone,' he said. 'You are no great weight and neither am I, so I will ride a horse with you. We'll do all we can to make it easy for you . . . '

He paused wearily, then added: 'I never thought I'd be so interested in your health, professor!'

8

The Avengers

There was a tinge of grey on the edge of the earth. It changed to silver-white, then to orange. Presently, the tip of the sun showed over the bare horizon.

It was dawn, July the eighth.

D'Aran released one hand from Daak's waist and looked at his compass. So far as he could calculate from dead reckoning they were following an accurate course for Sanna. And they could not be much more than a couple of miles away from the place. If the horses did not collapse, they would sight it very soon.

The horses . . .

They were one problem. They had drunk greedily of the salted water. And, as Daak had foretold, they had shown no immediate ill effect. But for the past two hours their hides had been twitching violently. Their mouths had turned white with foam. Occasionally they bucked and whinnied.

Daak . . .

He was another problem. D'Aran had to hold him in the saddle. He groaned with each jolt. Despite warnings, he had long since finished his water. D'Aran and Keith had watched longingly as he drank it. But they were glad that his thirst should be appeased. Everything depended on Daak.

But Daak was ill again. Very ill . . .

★　★　★

And in the fort . . .

A legionnaire who had not slept said to others who had not slept either: 'They must be there by now. It's dawn. D'Aran said they'd reach Sanna by dawn.'

'He said that they might — if the horses held out!'

'Never mind the horses. How about the pot-bellied professor! Is he holding out?'

'Still hours to wait . . . '

'God, I'm scared . . . '

'God, I'm thirsty . . . '

241

Keith's horse died when they were less than a mile from Sanna. It stopped suddenly, forelegs splayed. Then it rolled on its side. Keith only just managed to jump away in time.

D'Aran reined his own mount. He glanced at the professor and said: 'We'll have to carry him ourselves. If this animal collapses it will fall on Daak.'

Keith helped them to dismount. Daak could stand unaided, but no more. He was as weak as a baby and in pain. But he had not lapsed into one of his deliriums. He was, thank heaven, still clear headed.

In front they saw the tall steel tower, the roofs of the huts. They sensed the desolation.

Keith took Daak over his shoulder. For ten minutes he stumbled with the burden. Then he stopped. Not because it was D'Aran's turn to shoulder the professor. Not because he was unduly exhausted.

But because he saw the circle of barbed wire which surrounded the tower. And within the perimeter, the ruffled earth which could mean a minefield.

Slowly, Keith put the professor down. Then he said: 'How are we going to get through that?'

D'Aran was smiling. 'We are not, legionnaire, we are not! I think we might get through the wire, but the minefield, never. The area is a solid mass of buried explosives! *Dieu!* I should have thought of this. I should have known that such a place would be protected!'

Daak got on to his haunches. Then, holding on to Keith, he got upright. He blinked in the direction of Sanna. D'Aran explained to him. When he had finished the professor's oval face was palsied and glistening.

'You mean . . . I cannot get anywhere near the place!'

'That is so,' D'Aran said hoarsely. 'If we had mine detectors and wire cutters we might manage it — if we had three or four days to spare. But we have not three or four days, professor. It is now eleven o'clock. We have precisely four hours.'

'You must try to get through — make a path for me!'

'Quite impossible, professor.'

'Then we must get back!'

'On foot! Are you capable of such exertion?'

'But — but we'll die if we stay here. We're on top of the bomb . . . '

D'Aran laughed.

'We'll die if we run away. We would die if we were fifty miles from here. We might as well sit and wait. I suppose the end will be quicker for being closer.'

Daak's face crumbled. He wept . . .

Wept as they squatted on the sand.

Wept as the sun rose to its zenith.

He was weeping when the Arabs came.

★　★　★

The Bormone traders were justly outraged. One of their number had been killed in Fort Key. Others had been wounded. And why? Because they were making a simple investigation of a seemingly deserted fort.

It was infamy without precedent!

It called for revenge against legionnaires whom they had thought were friends. Yes, the Bormones told themselves, they may have to wait. But one day they would strike against the Legion. Only in a small way, of course. The days of the great tribal revolts were over. But they would kill at least one soldier . . .

Meantime, they rode towards the next village to sell their wares and tell of the outrage.

Their route took them through the Sanna Oasis.

They halted their horses and mouthed their astonishment when they saw the steel tower which had never been there before.

And the circle of cruel wire. And the empty huts.

But their puzzlement changed to fury when they saw the three figures squatting near the wire. Three men. Two of them in Legion clothing.

This was indeed the working of providence! The infidels had been delivered into their hands . . .

They loaded their muskets.

★　★　★

Keith saw them first. He nudged D'Aran. Together and without much interest, they watched the horsemen approach.

D'Aran said: 'We can't do anything to save them, either. But we may have company when we die.'

Keith was shading his eyes. He said: 'They look as if they mean business with those muskets . . . God! They do mean business! And I know why. I recognise some of them. They are the traders!'

Daak ceased weeping. The tears were dried by the impact of a new terror.

He screamed: 'They'll shoot us!'

'Almost certainly,' Keith assured him. 'But I don't suppose you have any very important plans for the future.'

Daak turned his face to the heavens in supplication. And as he did so, he became rigid. As though jerking himself out of a nightmare, he pointed to the southern sky.

'*Look! Look!*'

They followed the direction of his trembling finger. And at the same moment they heard a steady, droning sound. The sound of piston engines.

Then they discerned the plane. It was high in the brassy sky.

The tribesmen saw it at the same time. They halted uncertainly, for they had seldom seen such monsters. They decided to move away. Vengeance could wait.

But one of them decided otherwise. He was a young Bormone who had only lately acquired his musket. He wanted to use it. He aimed it at the kneeling figure of D'Aran then pulled the rusty trigger. As he rode after the others he saw a man fall and was satisfied.

A ball-shot had entered Daak's defective heart.

★　★　★

The plane was a light bomber. It dipped low over the proving ground while D'Aran and Keith waved. Then it swooped away to the north and disappeared.

'It's gone,' Keith whispered. 'They didn't see us . . . '

'It'll be back,' D'Aran said. 'It must come back. And I know why it is here.

247

There is only one explanation.'

'Yes? What is it?'

'It is making a final reconnaissance of the proving ground before the explosion. I think we are saved, *mon ami* . . . '

Five minutes later the plane landed and taxied towards them. The side door opened and a couple of baffled men in pale blue uniforms stood in the opening.

'*Sacre*!' one of them said. 'What are you doing? Where are you from?'

They did not answer until they were inside the plane.

Epilogue

The adjutant shook D'Aran's hand.

'Glad to see you back,' he said. 'You very nearly didn't come back.'

D'Aran nodded. There was nothing to say. The humiliation was coming now. This was merely a courteous preface.

'The explosion was successful, too — even though it had to be delayed a few days until we evacuated the area.'

Another nod.

The adjutant tapped his desk with his fingers. 'How old are you, lieutenant?'

'Er — twenty-two.'

'Twenty-two. A good age, *mon ami*. A good age to seek experience, don't you think?'

'Ah, *oui*, I suppose so.'

'With women, of course.'

Now it was coming! The old fool was trying to lead up to it gently! But inside himself, he'll be laughing, D'Aran thought. What does he know of temptation? He didn't have to fight for a scholarship to St.

Maixent! He'd never known poverty! He could meet a tramp like Lucinne every night and never suffer for it, as Lieutenant D'Aran was about to suffer!

The adjutant continued after a pause: 'But with the ladies one must use discretion.'

'I realise that — now.'

'Yet we all are indiscreet at times. We learn by our mistakes.'

Dieu! When was he going to reach the point? Why did the fool have to bleat platitudes. It didn't make it any easier.

'Sometimes we learn too late, major.'

'Perhaps. But not always. Anyway, it is an academic matter. Let us get down to business . . . '

He shuffled with some papers, putting them into precise order. Then: 'You will, I hope, continue with your appointment as treasurer of the mess funds.'

'I — I . . . '

'*Oui, I* thought you would, lieutenant. Now there is one other small matter. Strictly between ourselves, of course. It's about that fifty thousand francs you borrowed from me. Don't worry about it. Repay when it is convenient . . . '